The Full Color
Fairytale Book

by R.C. Scriven · illustrated by Andrew Skilleter

GRAMERCY PUBLISHING COMPANY

New York

Contents

9 Rapunzel

13 Rumpelstiltskin

16 The Babes in the Wood

21 Ali Baba and the Forty Thieves

27 Goldilocks and the Three Bears

29 The Monkey and the Spider

35 The Snow Queen

37 Little Red Riding Hood

41 The Keys of Summer

43 Hansel and Gretel

48 The Sleeping Beauty

53 Jack and the Beanstalk

57 The Frog Prince

61 The Golden Goose

65 The Clever Cook

69 Cinderella

75 The Return of Spring

79 Aladdin and the Wonderful Lamp

85 How to Catch a Leprechaun

89 King Grizzly Beard

Rapunzel

Long ago the king and queen of Bohemia had a darling baby daughter named Rapunzel. One day, when she was three years old, her father was out hunting in the forest with his hounds, huntsmen and horses. He began to chase a beautiful golden hind which started up from a thicket.

Now the deer was the pet of a wicked witch named Malgris and was the only creature in the world that she loved. As the hind began to flee, she mounted her broomstick, circled three times widdershins (witch-language for the wrong way round) and cast a spell over huntsmen, horses and hounds. And there they stayed, turned to stone, in the middle of the forest.

Then Malgris swooped on her broomstick over the royal palace, flew in at the open window of the nursery and seized Rapunzel.

Over the valleys, over the rivers, over the

mountains travelled the witch until, in a remote and secret part of the country, she came to a tall tower built of black stone. There was no door and only one window, which belonged to a solitary room at the very top of the tower.

In flew the witch and laid little Rapunzel on a bed in the middle of the room.

"There, child," she croaked, "here you are and here you will stay until you're sixteen." On a bedside table, next to the only chair, the witch left milk and honey, black rye bread and dried figs. Then she flew back out of the window.

Rapunzel cried and cried and cried, but nobody heard her. Night came and she sobbed herself to sleep. In the morning she spread some honey on the black rye bread and drank some milk. The whole day stretched before her with nothing to do and no toys to play with. Day after day, week after week, that was her life—to cry herself to sleep, wake, eat dried figs and bread and honey, drink milk and cry herself to sleep again.

From time to time, as the weeks lengthened into months and the months into years the witch flew in and left more food.

Eventually Rapunzel stopped crying and became resigned to her strange fate. She began to grow tall and slender and very beautiful. Her lovely golden hair grew longer and longer until it reached her waist and then her feet. It never stopped growing. To amuse herself, Rapunzel began to sing. She had a voice as lovely as that of a nightingale.

When spring came she let her golden hair float from the window, for she loved to feel the soft wind stirring it. But she did not know how beautiful she had grown, for there was no mirror in the tower, and she had long forgotten her father and mother. Only when the witch flew in the window did she vaguely remember being snatched from her nursery. Malgris never spoke to her. But she noticed that Rapunzel's hair was of exactly the same shade as the coat of the golden hind from the forest.

10

One day in spring when Rapunzel had let down her hair from the window of the tower and was singing, the sound of her voice came to the ears of Prince Felix, riding along in the woods. He reached the foot of the tower and called out, "Girl with the lovely golden hair and the still more golden voice, what is your name?"

"Rapunzel," replied the Princess.

"Rapunzel, Rapunzel," cried Prince Felix. "There is no door in this tall black tower."

"Then climb up by my golden hair," said the Princess.

So the Prince tethered his horse and climbed up into the room at the top of the tower where he fell instantly in love with the Princess.

Rapunzel began to tell him the story of the wicked witch who had carried her off when she was a child.

"You must never stay with me after sunset," she warned him. So before sunset the Prince duly climbed down again. But the next day, and the next he came again.

They were so happy laughing and talking that one evening at the end of a month, a week and a day, Prince Felix did not notice the sun was setting.

"You must go!" Rapunzel cried suddenly. "The witch is coming! Quick! Slide down my hair."

The Prince slid to the ground. But he was too late. The witch had seen him. She flew into the room on her broomstick and cut off all Rapunzel's golden hair with a pair of shears. Then she tied the long shining tresses to a hook and hung them out of the window.

Next morning, when the Prince came to the foot of the tower, Rapunzel tried to warn him. But her nightingale voice died in her throat. The Prince had almost reached the sill of her window when the hook gave way and he fell. He plunged headlong into a briary bush which had sprung up under a spell cast by the witch, and the thorns blinded his eyes.

As he groped his way into the forest, Malgris watched and cackled with laughter.

A year, a month, a week and a day passed by and the witch returned to the tower.

"Today you are sixteen," she told the Princess, "and my power over you is ended." And she placed the Princess on her broomstick and flew her down to the ground.

"Be off," said Malgris, "and good riddance."

Weeping, Rapunzel, her lovely hair shorn close, wandered into the wild, green woods. She lived on berries and drank the pure water of springs and streams. Once, she found honey from a wild bees' nest in the hollow of a dead tree trunk. At night she huddled herself among the dead leaves at the foot of some great forest tree. She thought always of her lost prince.

One evening, as she was making her bed of leaves among the gnarled roots of a huge oak, she heard a nightingale begin to sing as the moon rose. Rapunzel felt her heart swell and she began to sing back to the nightingale.

Her thrilling voice reached the ears of the blind prince, wandering sadly through a moonlit glade, unable to tell night from day. Joyously, he stumbled towards the golden sound.

"Rapunzel," he cried.

"Felix!" replied Rapunzel.

She ran to him, exclaiming "Oh, my love, my love" and put her arms around him. As she began to rain tears of love and sorrow over the Prince's upturned face, the warmth of her tears healed his eyes: he saw the face of Rapunzel leaning over him in the moonlight.

At last the spell of the wicked witch was entirely broken, and, hand in hand, the Prince and Rapunzel made their way over the mountains, over the valleys, over the rivers until they reached the Prince's own country. And there they married amidst the rejoicings of all the people.

As for Malgris, she had kept a tress of Rapunzel's hair and when she was finally caught, it was used to bind her to the stake where she was burned by the foresters—a fate she richly deserved.

Rumpelstiltskin

Once upon a time a poor miller had a daughter who was so beautiful that she became the talk of the whole neighbourhood. Everybody admired her. When she was sixteen, the mayor of the town asked her to become his wife but she refused for he was old, bald and ugly. So, out of spite, he invented the story that she could spin gold from straw.

Such a remarkable thing came to the ears of the King and he ordered the miller to bring his daughter to court. When the King saw the girl he fell in love with her at once. But he did not tell her so. Instead, he locked her up in a high room in a tower which contained bales and bales of straw and a good strong spinning-wheel.

"See that you complete the work by morning or I shall have you publicly drowned in your father's mill pool," he said.

"But I can't spin straw into gold, my lord," replied the girl.

"Nonsense, nonsense," said the King. "Everybody in Hohenzollen knows perfectly well that you can. Set about it, girl."

The miller's daughter began to weep bitterly. Suddenly, there was a puff of green smoke, out of which hopped the oddest little man she had ever seen. His head was as huge as his body was small. He had a great knobbly forehead and bushy eyebrows, but he was even balder than the mayor, and far older and uglier. He bowed to the miller's daughter.

"Don't weep, m'dear," he said. "I can spin straw into gold. By the hour. What will you give me if I spin this straw for you?"

"My necklace, sir," answered the miller's daughter. "I inherited it from my great grandmother and it's made up of moonstones, pearls and opals. If you wear it round your neck it will ward off coughs, colds and the evil eye."

The strange little man clapped his hands and capered in delight.

"For such a necklace I'll gladly spin this straw into gold," he said.

So the miller's daughter snuggled into the only armchair in the room and watched the dwarf set the spinning-wheel whirring. The sound was soothing and quite soon she dropped off to sleep.

When the first rays of the dawn sun crept through the chintz curtains, the girl awoke. There on the floor was a great heap of spun gold. The odd little mannikin had vanished.

There was so much gold that it took one of the King's strongest men all his time to carry it to the treasury. Naturally, the King was overjoyed. He ordered two waggon-loads of straw to be off-loaded into a larger room and told the miller's daughter to spin more gold by the following day or she would be ground between her father's millstones.

Again the poor girl wept. And once more there was a puff of green smoke, out of which the strange little man jumped.

"What will you give me if I spin this lot into gold?" he asked.

"Oh, sir, the ring from my finger. It was given to my mother by her fairy godmother. One touch of it cures chilblains, mumps, whooping cough and the mulligrubs."

"Splendid!" he cried. "I suffer painfully from the mulligrubs, in spasms. It's a bargain."

Again the whirr of the spinning-wheel soothed the miller's daughter to sleep. And again, when dawn peeped into her high room in the tower there was a vast heap of spun gold on the floor and the little man had vanished.

This time it took two of the King's strongest men to manhandle the gold into the treasury.

Delighted, the King ordered three waggon-loads of straw to be brought to a still larger room.

"Spin the lot by tomorrow morning," he said "or you shall be ground into flour, kneaded and baked in the mill kitchen."

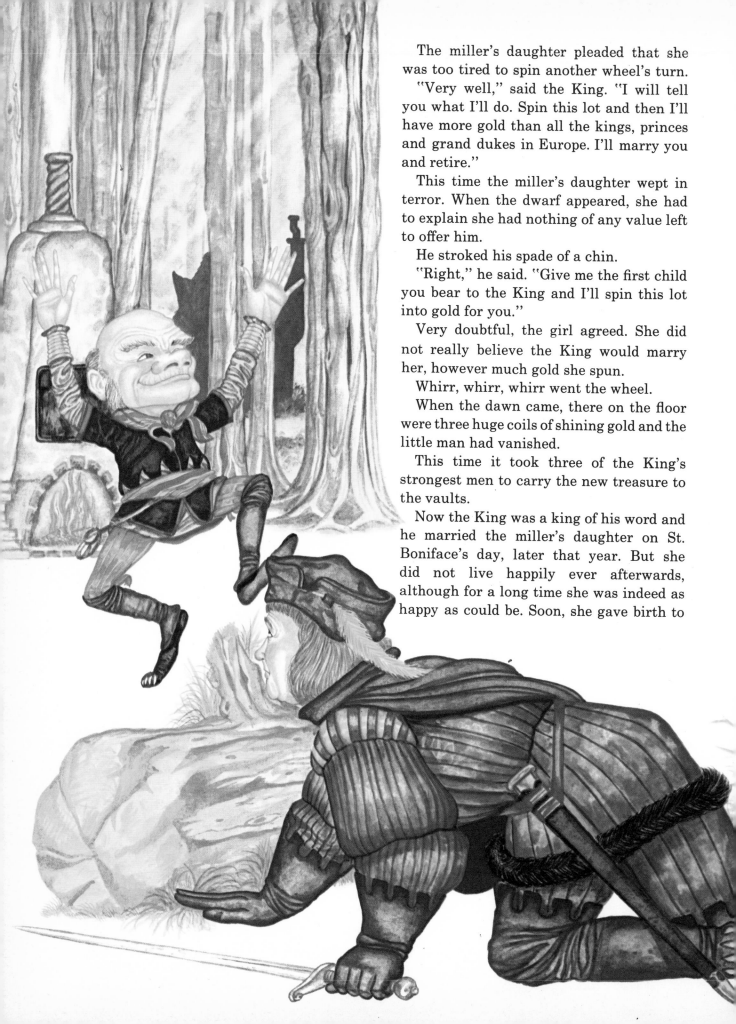

The miller's daughter pleaded that she was too tired to spin another wheel's turn.

"Very well," said the King. "I will tell you what I'll do. Spin this lot and then I'll have more gold than all the kings, princes and grand dukes in Europe. I'll marry you and retire."

This time the miller's daughter wept in terror. When the dwarf appeared, she had to explain she had nothing of any value left to offer him.

He stroked his spade of a chin.

"Right," he said. "Give me the first child you bear to the King and I'll spin this lot into gold for you."

Very doubtful, the girl agreed. She did not really believe the King would marry her, however much gold she spun.

Whirr, whirr, whirr went the wheel.

When the dawn came, there on the floor were three huge coils of shining gold and the little man had vanished.

This time it took three of the King's strongest men to carry the new treasure to the vaults.

Now the King was a king of his word and he married the miller's daughter on St. Boniface's day, later that year. But she did not live happily ever afterwards, although for a long time she was indeed as happy as could be. Soon, she gave birth to a child, a prince as handsome as his mother was beautiful.

By now the Queen had quite forgotten about the dwarf and her strange promise. But he did not forget. When the baby Prince was three months old the little man appeared while the Queen was eating bread and honey—and he demanded the child.

The Queen broke down utterly. She offered him her crown, all the jewels her husband had given her and all the gold the dwarf himself had spun for her.

"The child, the child," he repeated stonily. "My oven is hotting up already. The child."

The Queen beat her forehead on the ground and wept her heart out. At last the little mannikin was moved.

"If you find out my name in three days time, you may keep the child," he said. "I shall come back each night to give you three guesses. But if you don't know my name, the child must be mine." And he vanished.

The Queen sent messengers all over the kingdom to search out the name of the dwarf. But with no success.

When he returned on the first night she tried him with such names as Bagoribs, Wuggle-ears, Devil's tail.

The dwarf capered with glee.

"No, no, no," he cried.

The second night he returned again.

"Is it Pinch Me?" said the Queen.

"No, it is not."

"Clacketty-Brunen?"

"No, no."

"Oddletoes?"

"No, no, no." And the dwarf capered even more gleefully. "I'll build up my oven," he laughed.

On the third and last day, a weary messenger was returning desolately to the palace. He had travelled further than anyone else, but with no more success. Then he noticed a great fire burning outside a humpetty-dumpetty cross-grain cottage. Round the fire, which was built under a great stone oven, capered and skipped a dwarf with an enormous head and legs as thin as a black spider's. He had a great, knobbly forehead and bushy eyebrows and he was balder and uglier than the mayor of Hohenzollen. He was singing.

"Ha-ha-ha, hee-hee-hee,
  What's my name, asked the Queen, asks she?
  By snake's tongue, bat's wing, fire's flame
  Rumplestiltskin is my name."

The messenger crept away and then ran like the wind for the palace.

That night the dwarf stepped out of his puff of green smoke into the Queen's presence.

"What is my name?" he howled, rubbing his hands.

"Palimpsests?" asked the Queen.

"No," bellowed the dwarf.

"Poker-Pie?" asked the Queen.

"No," howled the dwarf. "Give me the child."

"Rumplestiltskin!" cried the Queen triumphantly.

In a fit of black rage the dwarf stamped the marble floor so hard that his foot went through and was trapped. Mad with fury, Rumplestiltskin seized his free foot and tugged at it. In fact he tugged it so hard that he tore himself quite in two. And that was the end of him!

So the Queen and her husband and their son the Prince lived happily ever after.

The Babes in the Wood

Long ago, in the days of the crusades, there were two children named Jack and Joan who lived in Yorkshire. Their mother had died when they were very young and their father was a knight in the King's service. He was one of the many Christian soldiers from all over Europe who had left their homes and families to fight in Palestine against the Arabs to save the holy city of Jerusalem from Moslem rule. The knights were often away on these crusades for many years and Jack and Joan's father had left them in the charge of his old and faithful servant, Henry.

Two years later, word came that the knight had been slain in battle before the walls of Acre. The children wept bitterly, but Henry said: "I'll protect you. Everyone in the castle will look after you. You must continue your schooling and do your sums carefully. Take courage."

Jack and Joan did as Henry told them. They studied hard in their schoolroom, which looked out over the castle garden. Their friends were the robins. In winter the children fed them with crumbs, while in the summer the robins sang to them as they worked.

One day the sentry on the castle wall heard the sound of a trumpet and saw three

16

people riding towards the castle—two men and a woman.

"Lower the drawbridge!" yelled the first man, who was short and fat.

"And be quick about it!" shouted the second one, who was lean and tall.

"Who are you?" asked the sentry.

The lady, who wore a golden gown and a steeple hat with a floating veil, said, very sweetly: "I am the sister of my poor dead brother—the children's aunt. These are my brothers, their uncles. We have come to look after our poor nephew and niece."

Jack and Joan rushed forward as the drawbridge was lowered. The lady dismounted and said: "My name is Dame Vivienne. I am your dear, dear aunt, come to take the place of your mother."

"Nobody can take mother's place," replied Joan.

"We are your uncles, Jeroboam and Rheoboam," said the two men, "and we have come to take the place of your father."

"Nobody can take the place of our father," replied Jack.

"How dare you speak with such impudence!" cried Dame Vivienne. "I can see we have not come a day too soon. You shall be scolded and whipped until you learn your manners."

After that, the three of them took possession of the castle. Dame Vivienne fingered the ribbon hangings and the rich tapestries on the walls. Jeroboam and Rheoboam rubbed their hands as they inspected the treasure chests. And that night the children were sent early to bed with nothing but bread and water for supper.

The intruders feasted merrily in the great hall. The children, shut away in their great cold bedroom, lay in each other's arms as they heard, floating up the chimney, the voices of the wicked uncles plotting with Dame Vivienne to ride out with them in the morning and lose them in the great forest.

"Joan," said Jack "we must fill our pockets with breadcrumbs. I have a plan."

In the morning each of the wicked uncles placed a child in front of him on his saddle

and rode off into the forest. They rode and rode all day until, deep in the forest, it was already night. Then they put Jack and Joan down and rode off, whooping with laughter. They had not noticed that, as they galloped along, Jack had secretly dropped a handful of breadcrumbs every few yards.

When the wicked uncles had ridden away Jack said: "Dear Joan, we can find our way back to the castle by following the bread-crumb trail. When we get there, Henry,

father's steward, will surely listen to our story and throw these horrible people out."

So they slept in each other's arms at the foot of a forest tree and at the first peep of dawn started to look for the breadcrumb trail. But they searched in vain: the birds of the forest had eaten every crumb.

Lost, forlorn, the children wandered hand in hand farther into the wood.

Meanwhile, in the castle, the wicked ones were gloating over their own clever-

ness. Rheoboam opened the treasure chest and Jeroboam took out moneybag after moneybag full of jingling golden coins. They sat down at a huge oak table and Rheoboam began to count.

"One for you and two for me, one for you and two for me," he chanted.

"And three for me, three for me," crowed Dame Vivienne.

The robins listened on the windowsill.

"We must find the children," they sang.

"Yes, yes, find the children."

Off they flew into the wood, and at sunset they found poor Jack and Joan. They were huddled in each other's arms with their eyes shut. Their faces were as cold as death.

A golden brown leaf blew from one of the great beech trees and came to rest over Joan's lips. The leaf did not stir and the robins sighed:

"She is dead, she is dead. And Jack is

dead. In winter the children gave us crumbs. In summer we sang as they did their sums.''

So the robins gathered hundreds of leaves in their beaks and covered the children with a blanket of gold and brown and scarlet. Then they flew sorrowfully back to the castle.

There a quarrel had broken out between the two wicked uncles and their sister.

''You've cheated,'' shouted Dame Vivienne. ''Those three gold pieces are mine.''

''Rubbish sister!'' yelled Rheoboam. ''Two of them are mine.''

''Oh, are they!'' yelled Jeroboam.

His great hand swept every gold piece on the table into a huge feathered hat. The two men started up and drew their swords. Dame Vivienne shrieked with laughter and scooped more coins and jewels into her apron.

While they were quarrelling and fighting among themselves, the sound of a trumpet suddenly rang out from beyond the castle walls, striking echoes from its old stones and penetrating its innermost rooms.

Old Henry, the steward, who had been terrified by the intruders, recognized the note of the trumpet at once and sprang to lower the drawbridge. Over it rode a knight in shining armour. The steward beat his breast as he told his lord and master what had happened.

''The story of my death in battle was false,'' said the knight. ''As false as the hearts of my two brothers and my even more wicked sister.''

And so he drove them out of the castle with the flat of his sword. Then, hardly knowing which way to look first, he mounted his horse. As he tried to decide where to search, the robins came circling above him, and, flying on before him, they at length led him to where the children were buried under the leaves. The covering made by the robins had warmed the children back into life and they woke to find their father stooping over them with tears of joy.

So the story of the Babes in the Wood ended happily after all, as every good fairytale should.

Ali Baba and the Forty Thieves

There lived in Baghdad, in the days of the great Caliph Haroun al Raschid, a certain merchant by the name of Ali Baba.

For a merchant, Ali Baba was a poor man. He had only one donkey, called Abdullah, and one slave-girl, Yasmin. Yasmin was the bane of his life. If he ordered her to do this, she did that. If he ordered her to do that, Yasmin always did the other.

"Yasmin, Yasmin," cried Ali Baba. "I ordered you to fill Abdullah's saddle packs with apricots. What did you do? You stuffed them with dates. You know as well as I do that there are date-palms all over the place and very few apricot trees. You'll be the ruin of me, girl."

"You don't listen to the talk of the bazaar," said Yasmin. "I do. Everyone's saying that the date-palms have been smitten, doubtless by the will of Allah, with a mysterious disease which makes the dates wither. Equally by the will of Allah, this year there is a more abundant crop of apricots than even the oldest man in Baghdad can remember. In a corner of your miserable warehouse I found three sacks of dates. I'll make your fortune, Ali, in spite of yourself. Leave it to me."

Secretly delighted by her cleverness he said, grumbling, "What's the use of a fortune? Were I as rich as in fact I'm poor, the Forty Thieves would soon plunder me."

"Be off with you," replied Yasmin. "I've more wits in my little finger than the Forty Thieves have in their forty thick skulls."

So Ali Baba set forth from the Damascus Gate, walking beside his donkey.

They went into the hills. Half an hour before noon, in a narrow gorge of mountains, Ali sought the shade of a great cedar tree. He tied Abdullah to a low branch and man and beast settled down to pass the hour of midday heat. Ali dozed off to sleep.

He was awakened by the sound of a trampling of feet and men shouting to one another. Forty mules, each loaded with an enormous oil-jar, went by, each mule led by a man armed to the teeth.

"The Forty Thieves," Ali whispered to himself in terror.

When the leading mule came to a boulder at the foot of a steep cliff, the leader yelled: "Open, Sesame." At once the boulder rolled aside and the whole train of men, mules and oil-jars filed into a huge cave which had appeared in the mountain-side.

Ali was too terrified to move. In half an hour the Forty Thieves reappeared. But now the oil-jars had disappeared and each thief was riding one of the mules. The clatter of their hooves sent small stones rolling down the hillside. As the last mule appeared, its rider shouted: "Close, Sesame." The boulder rolled back into place.

Ali lay still until the last sound had died away. Then he plucked up his courage and called: "Open, Sesame."

With a grinding sound, the boulder rolled from the mouth of the cave and Ali went cautiously in.

He found himself surrounded by heaps of silks and piles of gold, silver and jewels—the loot of years of robbing and plunder. The forty oil-jars made a hollow sound when Ali rapped them. Hastily, he helped himself to handfuls of jewels and fled. As he left, he called over his shoulder "Close, Sesame", as he had seen the last thief do. The rock rolled obediently back into place.

Ali untethered Abdullah and returned to Baghdad. He told his story to Yasmin.

"I don't believe it," she cried.

But when Ali showed her the handful of jewels he had brought back, she realized that he had indeed made an important discovery.

"Give them to me," she said. "I will go and sell them in the Street of the Jewel Dealers in the bazaar. I can get a far better price for them than you can. If anyone asks me where I got them, I'll tell them that they were given to me by my friend, the Caliph's head slave-girl."

With part of the money Yasmin bought two fine horses, and next day she and Ali Baba rode to the cave of the robbers. The rock rolled back at Ali's command and the two explored by the light of pinewood torches. Yasmin was in the seventh heaven trying on first one jewelled bracelet, then another.

"Hurry up," urged Ali. "Make up your mind which you want."

"This," she said. "No, that. No, I'll have the other."
Suddenly they both heard the sound of approaching hoofbeats.

"Hide, hide," cried Ali.

They managed to crouch behind some huge bales of silks just in time. In rode the Forty Thieves.

"Now, brothers," cried their leader, "the time is near when we can double our treasure and double it again. We'll raid the treasure house of the Caliph himself. This is the plan. In three days time it will be the dark of the moon. We'll enter Baghdad in broad daylight, disguised as honest merchants. Each of us will lead one mule. Each mule will be loaded with one oil-jar. The jars will be empty. But—ho, ho—the guards won't know that."

"Ho, ho, ho," roared the others.

"I've bribed the head porter," continued the leader. "He'll open the courtyard gate and let us in. We'll unload the empty oil-jars and we'll stable the mules in the Caliph's own stables. Then each of us will hide in an oil-jar. At midnight the head porter will unlock the door of the Caliph's treasure

house . . . and then . . . and then . . ."

Laughing, the Forty Thieves filed out of the cave on their mules. The leader shouted: "Close, Sesame." The rock rolled back, leaving the cave in darkness.

Yasmin and Ali waited a long time. Then Ali commanded the rock to open. They untethered their horses from the branches of the cedar where they had left them hidden, shouted "Close, Sesame", and rode back to Baghdad.

"Leave the rest to me," cried Yasmin.

On the day when the moon would be dark, Yasmin told her story to the Caliph's head slave-girl, who told the tale to the Caliph. He stroked his beard.

"You have done well, slave-girl. I will prepare a fine reception for these Forty Thieves."

In the narrow, teeming streets of Baghdad few people took any notice of so ordinary a sight as a train of forty mules loaded with oil-jars. The supposed merchants were admitted to the forecourt of the palace by the keeper of the gate without any difficulty and the Forty Thieves were safely hidden in their jars long before the last thin crescent of the moon began to sink. They knew they had a long time to wait before midnight came. They kept very quiet.

In the Caliph's enormous kitchen, however, all was bustle and activity. Instead of preparing a meal, the coals were bringing forty great iron cauldrons of oil to boiling point. Then each cauldron was carried into the courtyard by two of the Caliph's fighting men.

On a balcony overlooking the courtyard, Yasmin and Ali Baba watched silently with the Caliph. Just before midnight, torches flared to light all round the courtyard and a cauldron of boiling oil was tipped suddenly into each jar by the fighting men.

The end of the Forty Thieves, though painful, was quick.

Ali Baba was loaded by the Caliph with great riches. He became the greatest and most important of all the merchants of Baghdad and lived happily ever after with the clever slave-girl whom he freed and married.

And what became of the treasure of the Forty Thieves? The Caliph himself rode out to the secret cave and pronounced the magic words: "Open, Sesame."

And if you want to know what happened to the treasure then, why, you must ask the Caliph about that.

Goldilocks and the Three Bears

Once upon a time and a long time ago, there were bears all over Europe. This was because there were forests all over Europe, too. And bears love forests. In winter, all the bears went to sleep. In spring they woke up very hungry.

Now it so happened that one family of bears, Father Bear, Mother Bear and Baby Bear, who lived in the Black Forest, woke up particularly hungry, for the winter had been long and cold.

"I'm hungry," roared Father Bear.

"So am I," wailed Baby Bear.

"Patience," said Mother Bear. "There's nothing like porridge to satisfy hungry bears."

"Porridge with treacle," shrieked Baby Bear.

"Patience," repeated Mother Bear. "You can't expect me to make porridge in a flash. Father Bear, make the fire."

So Father Bear built a fire of little twigs, big twigs and logs. Mother Bear hung the cooking pot on a hook over the fire and began to stir in oatmeal with a bearish pinch of salt.

"Stir it with this wooden spoon, Baby Bear," she said. "No, no, no. Not madly, like that. Slowly, like this."

As the fire blazed hotter and hotter, the porridge began to bubble and boil. Baby Bear stirred it more and more slowly.

"That's about right," said Mother Bear. She poured the porridge into three bowls, a great big bowl, a not very big bowl and a very small one.

"Put them on the table, Father," she said. "We'll all go for a short stroll in the forest while the porridge cools a bit."

"I won't lock the door," said Father Bear. "We shan't be gone long."

Almost as soon as the three bears had set off, a small girl called Goldilocks came tripping along one of the forest paths. Now Goldilocks was usually a good child, but she had one fault that was always getting her into trouble: curiosity. She was always poking and prying into everything, especially if it looked secret or important.

Goldilocks saw that the front door of Bear House was open. And she had a perfectly horrid idea. She lifted the latch of the

garden gate, ran up the path and went straight into the house, without so much as ringing the bell and asking: "May I come in?"

In the sitting-room Golidlocks found three chairs. First of all she tried to sit in the great big chair but it was far too big to be comfortable. Then she tried the not very big chair, but that was too soft. Lastly she tried the very small chair, which was exactly right.

Goldilocks might very well have gone to sleep, but soon she smelled a most delicious smell, and she went into the kitchen to see what it was. She sat down in front of the great big bowl of porridge and tasted it, but it was so hot it nearly burned her tongue. Then she tasted the not very big bowl, but the porridge was not hot enough. So she sat down and tried the very little bowl and the porridge was so marvellous that she laced it with treacle and gobbled up the lot.

Then Goldilocks went upstairs. She found a great big bed and tried that, but it was much too hard. So she bounced on the not very big bed, but that was too soft.

"Oh, dear," said Goldilocks aloud to herself. Then she spotted the very small bed. The sheets were turned back, and, without taking off her nice yellow frock and green shoes, she scrambled into the bed. It was so exactly right that she closed her eyes and in a trice she fell fast asleep, her golden curls moving gently as she breathed peacefully.

Meanwhile the three bears were strolling through the forest, sniffing the new spring smells, and greeting all the animals they had not seen since the autumn before.

A squirrel ran up a beech tree and made a face at Baby Bear and Baby Bear put out his tongue. Then a jay shouted: "Go back, go back."

"He's right," grunted Father Bear. "The porridge should be cooled now, my dear."

So Father Bear and Mother Bear each took one of Baby Bear's paws and he swung between them back to Bear House. They all went into the sitting-room.

"Who's been sitting in my chair?" roared

Father Bear. "The cushion's on the floor."

"Who's been sitting in my chair?" moaned Mother Bear. "I know I left my spectacle case there, and where is it?"

"Who's been sitting in my chair?" cried Baby Bear. "Somebody has left the spectacle case there."

They trooped into the kitchen.

"Who's been eating my porridge?" boomed Father Bear. "Somebody's drowned it in milk."

"Who's been eating my porridge?" said Mother Bear. "It's swimming in treacle."

"Who's eaten all my porridge up?" screamed Baby Bear. "Whoever it was has licked the spoon dry."

The three bears were quite alarmed by this time, and, without looking for more clues, they clambered hastily upstairs to see if any damage had been done there.

"Who's been sleeping in my bed?" bellowed Father Bear. "The quilt's on the floor."

"Who's been sleeping in my bed?" wept Mother Bear. "The sheets are crumpled and where's my nightdress case?"

Then Baby Bear squealed: "Who's asleep in my little bed?"

The three bears gathered round the little bed, staring at the sleeping, golden-headed girl.

Goldilocks woke up and her big, big blue eyes opened wide in alarm. She sprang out of Baby Bear's bed and tangled the sheets round Mother Bear's feet. She dodged Father Bear's big clumsy paw and ran like the wind downstairs. Half a dozen rabbits ran in and out between Goldilocks and the three bears, who of course rushed out behind her.

Goldilocks fled out of the garden gate and along the forest path and almost, but not quite, out of the fairytale. For it's only fair to say that Goldilocks became very, very good after that, and never went into other people's houses without ringing the bell, or sat in other people's favourite chairs without asking, or ate other people's food. So she lived very happily ever after.

The Monkey and the Spider

There's no lovelier sight in the beautiful country of Italy than the bay of Naples and the Neapolitan people who live there are among the gayest people in the world. They love to sing, they love to dance and they adore music.

No wonder, then, that Guiseppe, the organ grinder, led a happy and comfortable life. With his barrel organ, or hurdy-gurdy, he took music into all the little streets and squares for a mile around his old, roomy, shabby house in the Street of the Ice-Cream Makers, overlooking the bay.

With Guiseppe lived his darling granddaughter, Carlotta. She was as darkly beautiful as her own shadow when she danced in the golden sunlight to the music of the hurdy-gurdy and her feet moved as gaily as the tossing waves.

On high days, feast days and holidays the Neapolitans showered pennies into the hat Guiseppe handed round as soon as he stopped grinding away at the handle of his hurdy-gurdy.

But alas, tastes change, even in Naples. Gradually fewer and fewer pennies were dropped into Guiseppe's hat. Carlotta's dancing was as lively as ever but fewer and fewer people clapped and nobody now cried: "Brava, brava!"

"We have become poor, Carlotta mia," said her grandfather one day. "There is nothing in the house but a crust and a handful of grapes. Now tomorrow is the feast of the Little Flower, so we must make a special effort. I will grind away twice as hard at my hurdy-gurdy. You must dance like a wave of the sea."

"Oh, I will," said Carlotta.

But next day, in the Square of the Fountains, the Neapolitans booed them both.

"Go away," they cried. "We watch the TV now." And they pelted Guiseppe and Carlotta with orange peel and hygienic Neapolitan ice-cream cartons.

Sadly Guiseppe stamped off with his hurdy-gurdy slung over one shoulder. Carlotta was weeping. As they passed through the Street of the Little Horses, she suddenly stopped.

"Grandfather," she cried. "Look. Signor Batista's pet shop. If we bought a monkey to hop and skip on the top of the hurdy-gurdy, maybe people would shower us with pennies again. Oh please, Grandfather."

"What do you think I am, Carlotta mia, made of money?" asked Guiseppe. But he went into the pet shop.

Signor Batista welcomed all customers with open arms.

"You want a baby crocodile?" he asked. "A zebra? Very expensive? A hippopotamus to float in your swimming-pool?"

"No," said Guiseppe.

"Oh, look, grandfather," cried Carlotta. "There's the most adorable little monkey. He looks so sad and miserable. His brown eyes are trying to speak to us."

"I can speak for myself," said the monkey suddenly, to the astonished Guiseppe and Carlotta. "Signor Batista is very cruel to me. He starve me. He beat me up. Buy me, buy me."

Guiseppe could not believe his ears.

"Monkeys can't talk," he cried.

"'Course they can't," said the monkey. "But Beppo can. Beppo is cleverer than a barrel-organ of ordinary monkeys. Buy me —and Beppo make your fortune."

"Grandfather, you must, you must," pleaded Carlotta.

"How much, Signor Batista?" asked Guiseppe, trembling.

"How much?" said Signor Batista. "Beppo is a bad, wicked monkey. He throws nuts at the other pets. He opens the cages and lets the crocodiles loose. I will give him to you with a pound of spaghetti."

The little monkey, unchained, leaped straight into Carlotta's arms, buried his

face on her shoulder and began to cry.

"Signor Batista wicked liar," he sobbed. "Beppo good monkey. Take me away."

So they took Beppo home to the shabby old house. The next evening Guiseppe slung his hurdy-gurdy over his shoulder and he and Carlotta went to the Square of the Fountains.

"Good people," said Guiseppe. "A wonder, a marvel—Beppo, the Talking Monkey. I grind the hurdy-gurdy, he dances and sings."

And he ground away at the handle of the barrel organ. But Beppo covered his eyes with his hand, hunched his shoulders and refused to dance.

"Boo," cried the Neapolitans. "Go away Guiseppe, you and your dumb monkey."

Guiseppe was very angry.

"When I get you home, I'll beat you," he shouted to Beppo.

When they did arrive home, Beppo leaped into Carlotta's arms.

"Don't let him beat poor Beppo," he sobbed bitterly. "Beppo frightened by people. Besides, Beppo need proper organ-monkey's uniform. A scarlet tunic. Yellow silk breeches. Silver buckled shoes and a little round pill-box hat with a jade green button on top."

"Impossible," said Guiseppe.

But Carlotta coaxed her grandfather into breaking into his life savings and they fitted up Beppo with everything he had asked for and a silver chain on a patent leather collar as well.

Next day, which was the Feast of St. Magdalena of the Golden Spinning-Wheel, they took Beppo, in his fine new uniform, to the Square of the Fountains. Guiseppe began to grind away a favourite tune.

Instantly Beppo began to prance and skip and shake his silver chain.

"Good people," he screamed. "Save me from my cruel master and his bad, bad granddaughter. They starve poor Beppo, they beat him black and blue."

"Wicked, wicked people," yelled the Neapolitans. "We'll give you black and blue!"

They pelted Guiseppe and Carlotta with banana skins, popcorn, hot dogs, ice-cream cartons, brandy-snaps and all the fun of the fair, including the hard balls thrown at the coconut shies and two of the coconuts themselves.

"You wicked, wicked, wicked monkey," cried Carlotta, when they were safely home. "No wonder Signor Batista was glad to give you away with a pound of spaghetti."

Beppo's teeth began to chatter.

"Chatter, chatter, chatter. It's not Beppo's fault," he sobbed. "Something comes over

31

me when they sing like that. Beppo's mind goes blank. Didn't I tell them how good and kind you and Guiseppe have been to me? I can't remember."

"Oh, yes you can," roared Guiseppe—and reached for his belt-strap.

With a loud scream, Beppo jumped out of Carlotta's arms, skipped up the dusty red velvet curtain, climbed the venetian blind and scrambled out of the window, which was open at the top.

Guiseppe caught the end of his silver chain and hauled him back again.

"Don't beat me. Don't. Don't," begged Beppo.

"I'm not going to," said Guiseppe. He fastened the end of the silver chain to the door knob.

"You stay where you are," he said. "Carlotta and I are going out to streets in Naples where nobody knows us. We will play the hurdy-gurdy for enough money to buy a bowl of spaghetti and a lump of goats' milk cheese. Behave yourself and maybe we will give you a piece of cheese when we come back. And don't touch my tobacco jar."

Guiseppe and Carlotta went out and locked the door behind them.

As soon as Beppo was alone he slipped out of the room. He opened all the drawers and threw their contents all over the floor. Then he caught Caterina, Carlotta's cat

and, grabbing her by the tail, swung her round and round his head. When he let her go, she streaked up the red velvet curtain and crouched on the curtain rail, spitting at him in Neapolitan, French, German and American—for Caterina was a much-travelled cat.

Beppo looked round to see what further mischief he could do. His beady brown eye was suddenly caught by the tobacco jar on Guiseppe's writing desk. It was a very handsome jar of black Etruscan pottery with the figure of a gay little Etruscan shepherd playing the pan-pipes and dancing merrily. On a rack beside it were three of Guiseppe's favourite pipes.

Beppo remembered that Guiseppe's last words had been to order him not to touch that tobacco jar. He chattered gleefully. Then he skipped onto the seat of Guiseppe's armchair and reached for the pipe rack. As he did so, he saw from the corner of one eye that the lid of the tobacco jar was moving very slightly up and down.

A small, hissing voice said: "You heard what Guiseppe told you. Leave this jar alone."

"Who are you? Where are you?" asked Beppo.

"Never you mind. I know who I am. And I know where I am. What's more I know where I come from. Which is more than you do, you miserable jungle creature."

Now Beppo was more full of curiosity than a whole pet-shop full of monkeys.

"Where do you come from?" he asked.

"Taranto," said the hissing voice.

"Pooh," chattered Beppo. "Taranto is a seaport on the coast of Italy. Everybody knows that."

"Indeed?" hissed the small, cold voice. "There's another thing about Taranto which not everybody knows."

"Tell me," said Beppo.

The voice did not reply, but the lid of the tobacco jar rattled.

Beppo snatched it off.

In a flash a big, black hairy spider with eight long, hairy legs darted out and bit Beppo in the heel.

"Tarantella, tarantella," hissed the spider, scuttling back into the tobacco jar.

Suddenly Beppo began to dance, and as he danced he sang:

"He or she, he or she
The Tarantella spider bites
Must hop and skip, jig and prance,
Waltz and wheel,
Toe and heel,
Stagger and reel
And dance, dance, dance
For seven days and seven nights."

When Guiseppe and Carlotta returned late that night they found Beppo dancing madly all over the floor, the chairs, the table. He danced on the tiled hearth, he danced on the mantleshelf, the window ledge, the knives and forks, the fire irons, on everything in sight. And as he danced, Caterina the cat, sat on top of the curtain rail and laughed and laughed and laughed until she fell off—fortunately onto the crimson cushion which Carlotta had sat on when she was a tiny child. Guiseppe and Carlotta began to laugh too.

"No need to tell me why you've made up your mind to dance for us," said Guiseppe. "Tomorrow you shall dance on top of my hurdy-gurdy and all Naples will flock to hear you sing the Tarantella song and shower the pennies into Guiseppe's hat."

And all Naples did.

The Snow Queen

Once upon a time there were two childhood sweethearts named Kay and Gerda, who lived in a small town of tall, wooden houses.

In each house the ground floor was overhung by the floor above, which, in its turn was overhung by the next floor. On the topmost floors the windows faced one another across the street so closely that the people who lived there could open their windows, lean out and shake hands—or if they happened to be quarrelsome, fists.

In the spring and summer Kay and Gerda played together in the fields and woods which surrounded the little town. When the deep snows of winter came, they wisely stayed indoors.

Every morning as soon as he woke up Kay would open his window and shout: "Gerda, Gerda."

Then Gerda would fling her window up and cry: "Good morning, Kay. Brr. Isn't it cold?"

"Never mind, Gerda," would come the reply. "It's lovely and warm indoors. I'm having porridge heated up on the stove for my breakfast. What are you having?"

"Herrings fried in oatmeal. I'll have to go now. Mother's calling. We'll open our windows and talk after breakfast."

One night a strong north-east wind blew and in the morning both children found that Jack Frost had made patterns of ferns and flowers on the window panes—strange beautiful patterns which prevented either of them from seeing across even the short distance from one window to the other.

So Kay put two pennies on a shovel over the stove and Gerda did the same over her stove. When the pennies were hot, they pressed their coins against the window from the inside and so melted two peepholes through which they could see each other.

How merry they were as they put out their tongues at each other and laughed and talked in sign language.

With hot pennies they melted larger and larger peepholes. Soon they were able to see not only the tall, narrow houses on the other side of the street, but the street itself, far below and covered from side to side by a great carpet of drifted snow.

Then Kay's eyes opened very wide. Along the street he saw a sleigh drawn by a team of six reindeer. Huge icicles hung from the wooden arch which divided the seat of the sleigh from the galloping animals. Driving the sleigh was the loveliest lady Kay had ever seen. She wore a crown that sparkled in the frosty sunshine. Her face was more beautiful than the dawn and colder than the snow. As her sleigh passed below, she looked up at Kay. And as she looked, an icicle seemed to stab his heart. She was the Snow Queen.

Without a word, Kay ran out of his warm room, down stair after stair and out into the street. The wind was icy, but he did not feel cold. The whole of his body was colder than the wind. The Snow Queen wheeled her reindeer team and drew up the sleigh beside him.

"Come," she said in a voice as crystal clear as the icicles. "Sit beside me, Kay."

The last that Gerda saw of her sweetheart was his ice-blue eyes staring unseeingly at her, and the snow rising like white smoke from the runners of the sleigh as it drove off like the wind towards the North.

"Kay, Kay, Kay," she called.

He never turned his head.

Her heart aching, Gerda muffled herself in her furs, took her snow-shoes from the cupboard and hurried down to the street.

At first, the tracks of the sleigh were easy to follow. But once Gerda was clear of the town she found the wind had smoothed out all trace of them.

The sky glittered with huge stars, for the midnight sun had gone down two months before. Gerda knew that the Pole star showed the true north and that the pointers of the Great Bear showed her the Pole. She went on courageously.

Though she was half frozen, weary and hungry, her love for Kay would not let her give up. Wild reindeer, pawing the snow, showed her where moss and sparse berries were to be found. These she ate. She melted snow in her hands and drank it to quench her thirst. For days Gerda went on and on. At night—which she only knew from day by guesswork—she slept huddled in her furs in the shelter of some boulder.

Then the northern lights began to flicker like the fire and sheen of diamonds—so confusing her that she could not tell where the Pole star was. An Arctic fox howled. It's voice seemed to say:

"This way. Gerda, keep on."

A solitary Lapp, driving a sleigh drawn by one reindeer gave her some rancid butter and a strip of dried reindeer meat and said:

"Go on, Gerda. North lies—there."

Last of all, when a snow storm sprang up and she thought she must surely perish in these wild wastes of Lapland, a grey lag goose came beating its wings around her.

Gerda took heart. She knew that the children of the grey lag goose are born without fear, for the grey lag nests further north than any other wild bird, beyond the reach of even the Arctic fox.

"Follow the beating of my wings," the grey lag called.

All day, all night, Gerda followed.

At last she saw a sight more wondrous even than the northern lights. Across the vast waste of snows stood the palace of the Snow Queen. Its towers and turrets and pinnacles flashed and glittered in the starlight like the crags of an iceberg, all the colours of the rainbow.

In one more day's journeying Gerda came to the palace and climbed its steps, cut in the snow.

No-one challenged her as she entered. And there, in the great hall, whose roof was supported by pillars of ice, the Snow Queen sat on her throne of wind-carved snow. Flickerings of magnetic light lit the throne room. And at the Snow Queen's feet . . .

"Oh, Kay, Kay, Kay," cried Gerda joyously.

Kay must have heard her, for he turned his head. But he looked at her with cold, blank eyes as though he were snow-blind. Then he turned his face away and looked at the Snow Queen.

"He is my slave," she said. "Go, leave my palace and perish in the waste of the end of the world."

Gerda held up her head and gave the lovely, cruel Snow Queen glance for glance. Then she ran forward and took Kay in her arms. She began to weep scalding tears of love and compassion.

Her tears melted the icicle the Snow Queen had planted in his heart.

"Gerda, Gerda," he cried. "I know you now. The sweetheart I have loved all the days of my life."

Her power broken at last, the Snow Queen fled from her palace behind her galloping reindeer. As she disappeared into the black night, the eastern sky began to flush a rosy pink and the rim of the sun appeared above the horizon. The long, polar night was over.

Kay and Gerda harnessed two reindeer to a sleigh lined with crimson velvet and, to the jangling of its bells, began their long journey back to the little wooden town. Years later, when they grew up and had long forgotten the Snow Queen, they married and lived happily ever after.

Little Red Riding Hood

Once upon a time there lived a prosperous woodcutter whose name was Franz. He had a beautiful wife called Truda and a daughter whose name was Mitzi. Mitzi was usually called Little Red Riding Hood, because of a brilliant scarlet cloak she wore. Franz was a good workman and supported his wife and daughter very comfortably. But Franz's old mother, a woman of a very independent spirit, chose to live by herself some distance away in a log cabin Franz had built for her.

One morning Franz said: "Wife, I've been thinking about my old mother. I have a feeling that she is running a bit short of the good things of life. But she's too proud to mention the fact. You know what the old lady's like."

"Indeed I do," said Truda. "As soon as you've gone to work I'll pack a few things in a basket and Little Red Riding Hood shall take them to her granny."

Franz kissed his wife and daughter, shouldered his axe and strode into the woods, whistling.

"Mother, what am I going to take to Granny?" asked Little Red Riding Hood.

"A pound of butter, darling. A pound of sugar, two of flour, half a pound of currants and a dozen big, brown eggs," replied her mother, "and a special cold pie I've made for her. Now put on your warm red riding hood, the one Daddy and I gave you for Christmas. Mind you take the things straight to Granny and don't stop to pick flowers by the way. The big bad wolf might be lurking about."

"I'll run ever so fast," Little Red Riding Hood promised.

"Mind you don't tumble and break those eggs."

"Oh, I won't," said Little Red Riding Hood and set off.

Now the big bad wolf *was* lurking about. He had been listening at the keyhole. He slipped off into the woods and as he could run very much faster than Mitzi, he ran straight to Granny's cabin and knocked at the door.

"Who's that knocking at my door?" called Granny.

"It's me, Granny. Red Riding Hood."

"Your voice sounds very hoarse."

"I've got a bit of a cold."

"Then don't stand there shivering and shuddering. Lift the latch and come in at once."

The big bad wolf lifted the latch with his nose and went in. Granny was sitting up in bed in her nightgown and warm red dressing gown, her nightcap tied under her chin and her reading glasses at the end of her nose. The big bad wolf immediately sprang at her and gobbled her all up—all, that is, except the dressing gown, the nightcap and the second best glasses.

Then he carefully put on the dressing gown, tied the nightcap under his hairy chin and perched the reading glasses at the end of his nose. Presently he heard Little Red Riding Hood trot along the path and knock at the door.

"Who's that?" he asked, though of course he knew perfectly well who it was.

"It's me, Granny. Red Riding Hood. I say, you do sound hoarse."

"I've got a bit of a cold, dear," said the wolf. "Open the latch and come inside."

"Good morning, Granny dear," said Little Red Riding Hood, opening the door. "I've brought you a basket of good things. Butter, sugar, flour, currants and a dozen speckled brown eggs, only I'm afraid one of them is a bit cracked. And a special cold pie mother made for you."

"Put the basket on my bedside table, dear," said the wolf.

"Shall I break the cracked egg into a saucer and beat it up with some milk and sugar? It will do your throat good."

"Not now, dear," said the wolf.

Little Red Riding Hood came closer and looked at the wolf with surprise.

"Oh, Granny, what big ears you have."

"All the better to hear you with," said the wolf.

"And Granny, what big eyes you have."

"All the better to see you with through my reading glasses," said the wolf.

"And oh, Granny, what big teeth you have."

"All the better to eat you with," snarled the wolf, with a horrible smile.

Little Red Riding Hood screamed.

"Wretched child," growled the wolf. "Stop screaming this instant and come here."

Little Red Riding Hood turned to run for her life.

The wolf threw the bedclothes to one side

and sprang out of bed. But he was not used to wearing a dressing gown and he tripped over its long hem. He tried to untie the strings of the nightcap with his front paws, but his paws fumbled clumsily and he pulled it down over his eyes, dislodging the reading glasses, and making it impossible for him to see at all.

Howling with rage, he tried to rush through the door. Instead he hit his head on the door post and knocked himself out. He fell in a heap on the floor.

Little Red Riding Hood, meanwhile, had run like the wind along the path leading into the forest.

Soon she heard the sound of an axe ringing down the glade.

"Daddy, Daddy, Daddy," shouted Little Red Riding Hood.

Franz came running towards her and snatched her into his arms.

"I'm all right," she gasped. "It's the wolf. He's in Granny's bed."

Just as the wolf rose dizzily to his feet Franz rushed into the cabin. With one mighty blow of his woodman's axe he chopped off the wolf's head.

To their surprise—and relief—there stood Granny, safe and well in her rather crumpled nightgown, blinking a little because she was very short-sighted without her glasses, and very bewildered indeed.

After Franz had dragged the wolf out by the tail and buried him, they all went back home. Little Red Riding Hood held tightly to his hand all the way back to the cabin.

I am glad to say that the little girl soon recovered her merry spirits. When she grew up she married the Prince's chief huntsman. The red riding hood of her childhood was carefully put away between linen sheets scented with lavender.

"It will be useful when our own little girl comes along and grows up a bit," she told her husband.

"By that time, my love," said the chief huntsman "I'll see to it that there isn't one big, bad wolf left in the whole of the forest."

And there wasn't.

The Keys of Summer

Holland, the Hollow Land, or the Low Land, got its name because so much of it lies below sea-level. Hundreds of square miles of rich pasture have been won from the sea by building dykes and dams. A flat, uninteresting land? Tell me, when you have read one of the most charming fairy tales in Europe.

In the days when the Hollow Land had almost as many windmills as it had bridges over canals, a certain spring had been late in coming. All winter Jan and his sister Margaretta had kept themselves warm by skating, like everybody else, on the frozen dykes.

Jan's big blue trousers and bright red jacket made blurred spots of colour against the snow. The wide, starched wings of Margaretta's Dutch head-dress seemed almost to lift her into the air as she raced beside her brother on her ringing skates.

It was mid-March before the ice began to melt. Sadly the children stored away their skates and put on the wooden clogs—so

clumsy-looking and yet so light. But still it was cold, and the east wind blew, hissing, over the Hollow Land.

It blew and it blew through March, through April, and on even as far as the beginning of May.

The red-and-white cattle, usually turned out into the fields to graze and gambol joyously over the first bite of new grass, were kept in their warm stalls. The haystacks built under the roofs of the big, red-tiled barns sank lower and lower.

Only cats, curled up in spotlessly clean kitchens were content, as what cat would not be, with peat fires and huge Delft saucers of rich, creamy milk.

Everybody else—men, women, children, dogs and cattle and horses—longed for the grey clouds to go and the gold sun to blaze again.

That year, even the tulips did not bloom as usual with the many-coloured flames of their petals.

"Oh, Jan," sighed Margaretta "the calendar says it's spring, but the east wind hisses: it is winter still."

"The real spring will come some day," said Jan sturdily. "Shall we play hide and seek?"

"No, Jan. I'm tired of all our games," replied Margaretta. "I know. All my dolls are in bed with coughs and colds and sneezes. You can be the doctor looking at their tongues and making them say 'Ninety-nine', while I give them mustard plasters and bowls of hot soup."

The days passed. The weeks passed. And still the clouds, like herds of grey elephants, lumbered endlessly along and there was no gleam of sun.

The first week of May came . . . the second. Then one Monday morning, Margaretta, bored and miserable, suddenly lost her temper and smacked all her dolls for not getting better. All at once she felt a great deal better herself and put them back to bed again.

"There, darlings," she said. "You're like mother. All you need to make you well and happy again is lots and lots and lots of sunshine."

"That's what everyone in Holland needs, my little Margaretta," said her father, who had overheard her. "You and Jan are looking as white as sticks of celery. You've been cooped up indoors far too long."

Big, handsome Dirk Thripp smiled down at his two children.

"Tell you what I'll do. I'll take you with me when I go out this afternoon to patrol Den Groot Dam."

The children clapped their hands. Den Groot Dam was the great sea-wall which protected that part of the coast from the grey-green waves of the Zuyder Zee.

"Wrap yourselves up warmly," advised Dirk.

One on each side they clung to their father's hands as he strode out along the line of the Groot Dam. The never-ceasing east wind hissed behind them. Sea birds swirled and whirled like snowflakes in the grey sky.

The air smelled of salt. Suddenly, Dirk stopped and pointed.

"Look, children."

Close inshore, her three masts set with tight-hauled sails, the children saw a magnificent ship.

"A merchantman. English, by the cut of her jib. Yes. I can read her name. *The Golden Vanity*."

The wind shifted a point or two and they all heard the sound of singing, in a tongue they did not understand, but which stirred their blood as they strained to listen.

"Oh, a ship have I got in the North
    Country
And the name of that ship is the Golden
    Vanity
And I fear she will be taken by the
    Spanish gallalee
As she sails by the lowlands low."

"She would not dare to hug the sea wall of the Groot Dam so closely," said Dirk "if the wind was a west wind. She's veering and tacking to work her way to the great port of Amsterdam. See how she rolls."

When they got home, the children told their mother about the incident.

"The west wind," she sighed. "God send the west wind with summer on its wings."

The very next morning Jan got up very early. He shouted to Margaretta: "Get up! Get up! There's a piece of blue sky big enough to patch my trousers. The wind's changed. It's warm and blowing from the west."

They ate a hasty breakfast of flat cake still smelling warm from the oven, and buttered with golden-yellow butter and spread thickly with the last of the clover honey. Then off they scampered, hand-in-hand, into the meadow just over the bridge of the canal.

Larks were singing their hearts out high in the sky which, minute by minute was becoming bluer and bluer.

Blackbirds, thrushes and linnets joined in the song of the larks. While the sails of all the windmills in sight sped round as merrily.

"Look, Jan. There's the first cowslip of the year," cried Margaretta. She combed the grass with her fingers feeling for the cool, hairy stem.

"There's another," cried Jan "and another and another."

Filled with happiness, they wandered across the meadow picking cowslips until they had picked enough to make a cowslip ball.

They did not hear the silent footsteps approaching over the grass. But a shadow, fainter than the shadows of the high, puffball clouds made them look up.

They saw a tall, most gracious lady. Honeysuckle was wreathed in her hair, which was of a darker gold. Her breath was sweeter than the breath of new-mown hay.

She said: "Cowslips are the keys of summer. And as you two are the first children who have found the keys of my palace this year you may open its magic doors and wander through it to your heart's delight."

So, hand in hand, they did.

Hansel and Gretel

Once upon a time there lived in the Black Forest a poor woodcutter whose name was Wilhelm. Poor though he was, he was happy with his beautiful wife and their two children: a boy, Hansel and a girl, Gretel.

Their mother died when the children were still quite young. For some time Wilhelm tried to look after them but found it very difficult to be both father and mother to them and carry on his trade as a woodcutter as well. He married again, thinking his new wife would look after them and love them as he did.

Unfortunately for the children, their stepmother soon showed herself in her true colours. She was both mean and cruel.

"How much happier I would be," she told herself, "if I could get rid of these children, who are only two extra mouths to feed."

She began to point out to Wilhelm how poor they were, how hard the times were.

"Besides," she added "it isn't fair to the children. They are beginning to grow up. If they didn't have us to consider, they'd soon make their own way in the world."

In the back room of the woodcutter's hut, Hansel and Gretel, each on a heap of rags, lay awake, listening.

"Tomorrow," continued their stepmother, "I have a plan to help them. You and I, Wilhelm, will lead them out into the forest and lose them. In this way they will learn to look after themselves."

"You know best, my dear," said Wilhelm. "Tomorrow I will do as you say."

"Hush, Gretel," whispered Hansel. "Pretend to be asleep."

He stole quietly into the forest, to a stream near their hut. He filled his pockets with small white pebbles and crept back into the hut.

In the morning the children were led far into the forest. Every few yards, Hansel let a white pebble drop. All day the wood-cutter worked in the clearing, cutting down trees and sawing their branches into neat blocks. As darkness fell, the children went to sleep under the shade of a great forest oak, and Wilhelm and the cruel stepmother crept away.

The singing of the birds awakened them at dawn. Gretel at once began to cry, but Hansel said: "We are not lost. Look."

And Gretel saw a white pebble at the edge of the clearing, then another and another. So they followed the trail and eventually arrived back at the hut.

The wicked stepmother pretended to be delighted by their safe return, but in the morning she said: "Today we're going out into the forest again."

There was no time for Hansel to gather more white pebbles from the brook. Instead, he filled his pockets with breadcrumbs. As they were taken deeper and deeper into the forest he dropped first one crumb then another.

The children played happily among the trees. They were careful to stay close enough to hear the sound of chopping and sawing, determined that this time they would not be left behind. Eventually, feeling rather hungry, and noticing that it was getting dark, they made their way back to the clearing where they could still hear the comforting "clunk" of the axe.

There was no-one to be seen! At first they thought they had lost their way, but, looking around in bewilderment, they soon discovered what had happened, and how they had been deceived.

The woodcutter had left his saw with its teeth in the trunk of a tree and the wind had made the blade twang.

"Father has left us," said Hansel. "Never mind. We can find our way home by the breadcrumbs I dropped."

When he began to look for the bread-

crumb trail, however, his heart despaired.
The birds of the forest had gobbled up all
the crumbs. They were utterly lost.

Hand in hand the children wandered
deeper into the forest.

"We shall die, Gretel," said Hansel
"unless we get out of this forest soon."

"Look," said Gretel, suddenly.

There, at the other side of a clearing,
was a most attractive hut. Its walls and
roof were made of gingerbread, with icing
on the tiles. The door was made of chocolate,
with a porch of twisty barley-sugar sticks.
There were marzipan windows, and the
smokeless chimney pot seemed to be made
from a thick stick of liquorice. There was a
mint humbug by way of a knocker on the
door.

"Come, Gretel," said Hansel, and he lifted
the knocker and banged.

"Come in," answered a sleepy voice.

In the kitchen beside a glacé cherry fire
sat a little old woman.

"Please," said Hansel, "We're lost in the
forest. My sister and I are hungry and
thirsty."

"Sit you down, my dears," said the little
old woman. She hobbled to a cupboard and
brought them two glasses of milk and a plate
of honey cakes. Hansel and Gretel began to
eat and drink—but immediately they felt
more lost than ever.

The old woman cackled with laughter.

"Now you are in my power," she said.
She began to rub her hands together. Her
fingers were long and crooked and yellow,
like crocodile's claws.

The children sat helpless under the magic
spell which had bound them as soon as they
had tasted the old woman's food and drink.
Her voice, high and thin, like sniggering
laughter, continued.

"I, Helga the witch of the wood am
hungrier than a famished cat."

She hobbled over to Hansel and began to
prod him and pinch him.

"H'm, y'm," she croaked. "You'll do,
when I've fattened you up."

Then she pinched Gretel.

"You're thin and active," she said. "Take
my broom, girl and set about sweeping out
the kitchen."

The witch then lifted down a large
wickerwork cage which hung from a hook
between the oven and the kitchen sink.
She opened the door, bundled Hansel inside

and locked it again with a key tied to her apron string.

Then with surprising strength she hoisted the cage back on to its hook between the oven and the kitchen sink.

Gretel, in turn, was compelled for a whole week to dust and sweep and polish and do all the drudgery of the kitchen.

What made her weep her eyes sore, though, was that she had to feed Hansel with all sorts of fattening food. Every day the witch put her crocodile claws between the bars of the cage and prodded and pinched poor Hansel to judge how plump he was becoming. Gretel, she starved.

On the eighth day the witch cooked a fine fat chicken in the oven and made Gretel feed it to Hansel.

"You're not fattening up, boy," she grumbled.

Now the hut was dark and the witch's eyesight not of the best, so she did not know that he was pushing out most of the food Gretel fed to him. But he did eat some of the chicken and he gave Gretel some, too.

Before she went to bed, the witch again put her hand inside the bars of the cage. But Hansel was too clever for her. He put into her groping fingers the thigh bone of the chicken.

"Wretched boy," said Helga. "You're getting thinner, not fatter. No matter. I'm getting hungrier and hungrier. I'll cook you in the morning."

Morning came, and the witch duly unlocked the cage and tied Hansel up.

"Go and open the oven door," she ordered Gretel. "Put your head and shoulders inside and see if the oven is hot enough to roast the wretched boy."

Gretel opened the oven door.

Now Helga intended to roast both of them, as she thought Hansel was not plump enough. Gretel paused.

"The oven is quite cool," she said.

"Then chop some more wood and heat up the oven," replied the witch.

Gretel did as she was told.

When the clock struck noon, Helga said: "Try the oven again."

Gretel made the oven door clang but did not put her head and shoulders inside.

"It's still only just warm," she said. "If you don't believe me, try for yourself."

"I will," said the witch.

As soon as her head and shoulders were inside the oven, Gretel used all her strength to push the witch inside and slammed the door. Then she cut Hansel free and both of them furiously stoked the fire. The wicked witch was roasted alive!

Meanwhile the combined heat of the big wood fire and the glowing oven began to melt the chocolate door and char the gingerbread walls and make bull's eye holes in the marzipan windows. And Hansel and Gretel escaped at last from the terrible gingerbread house, which had seemed so gay and attractive to them when they first saw it.

"We're still lost, though, sister," said Hansel.

Brave though she was, Gretel began to weep a little.

"You're not a coward, are you Gretel?" asked Hansel.

"N-n-no," sobbed Gretel.

"Tell you what then. There's a big chicken coop in the garden where the witch kept the chickens she used for fattening up her prisoners. Let's free the poor things."

So they opened the wooden door. Out rushed three or four half-starved chickens, squawking and flapping their wings for joy. They made such a rush to get out that Hansel laughed to see them. He laughed so much that he stumbled and upset the coop. As it tilted over they saw something underneath it that amazed them: a fair-sized oak chest with copper hoops and a padlock.

"A treasure chest!" cried Hansel.

"And the key's in the lock."

In the chest there were jewels and gold coins and pieces of eight galore. The excited children filled their pockets until gold and jewels bulged over the top.

Then they filled Hansel's concertina cap and Gretel's big floppy sunbonnet with pieces of gingerbread and broken-off sticks of barley sugar from the porch.

Hand in hand they set off through the forest, hoping to find a ranger or even an outlaw who could direct them to their home. Instead, they found a stream as clear as daylight, with pretty coloured pebbles over which the water danced and sparkled, and that night, full of gingerbread and with no fear of going thirsty, they slept under the shade of a great oak. The woodcutter's children were too wise to sleep under a beech.

"Father says the beech is the mother of the forest," said Hansel. "But she loves cold ground and nothing, not even moss grows under her shade. Let's follow the stream as soon as the sun rises. It's bound to lead us out of the forest in time."

So for three days and nights they rested and travelled. When they had eaten all the gingerbread, they lived very well on berries and clever Hansel found a few hoards of nuts, buried during the previous autumn and then mislaid by absent-minded squirrels.

At last they heard a sound which had been familiar to them all their lives: the ring of an axe-blade on wood. They followed the sound and it led them to where their father was felling a big pine tree. As Wilhelm saw them rushing towards him, he burst into tears.

"I've never had a night's sleep since I wickedly agreed with your stepmother to lose you in the forest," he said. "Your step-mother was duly punished. She died of eating a poisoned berry of deadly night-shade, in spite of my warning her not to. I've been searching for you in the forest ever since. I've managed to live on nuts and sweet berries."

"So have we," cried Hansel and Gretel.

They told him of their adventures and showed him what was making their pockets bulge.

Early next morning, all three set off from the forest and journeyed along the highway to the city, where they soon found merchants to buy the witch's jewels. And Wilhelm, Hansel and Gretel lived richly and happily ever after.

The Sleeping Beauty

Once upon a time, a girl child was born to the King and Queen of Bavaria. Great was their rejoicing, for they had waited in vain for seven years for a baby to arrive.

"My love," said the King, "we must invite all the fairy godmothers of the whole of Germany to the christening."

"Except Maultash," replied the Queen. "She is so ugly and wicked she would be more likely to put a curse on our child than to give her a blessing."

"How right you are, my love," said the King.

So he sent for his chief herald, Crispin, and ordered him to send out royal invitations to twelve fairy godmothers to come to the christening.

The cathedral was crowded for the great

occasion by old and young, rich and poor. The cardinal lord archbishop held the child in his arms. The twelve fairy god-mothers each held a lighted candle as the cardinal sprinkled holy water on the child's forehead.

"I name you Violet Rose," he said.

The baby laughed and gurgled and reached out her tiny hands to try to catch the pretty lights of the candles.

Then the twelve fairy godmothers gave Princess Rose their gifts.

"I give you beauty," said the first.

"Health," said the second.

"Wealth," said the third.

One by one, the others added such gifts as kindness of heart, courtesy, wisdom and truthfulness, hope and joy.

The twelfth was just about to add her gift when all the candles in the cathedral began to flicker. There was a sudden smell of sulphur and a cloud of black smoke darkened the aisle.

When it dissolved, everyone saw the wicked fairy, as ugly as a gargoyle.

"I, too, will give this child a gift," she cackled. "She shall indeed grow in beauty and goodness. But when her sixteenth birthday arrives, Princess Rose will prick her finger on the spindle of a spinning-wheel and drop down dead."

With a wild shriek of laughter, the wicked fairy disappeared in a flash of green light.

So great was the confusion that nobody heard the last fairy make her gift.

"The Princess shall not die," said the twelfth fairy. "When the curse comes on her she shall sleep instead, as the whole of the court shall, for a hundred years."

Next morning, the King called a meeting of the wisest men in the land.

"There is one certain way of averting the curse, Your Majesty," said the oldest and wisest man. "If all the spinning-wheels in the land are destroyed, how can the Princess prick her hand on the spindle of one?"

"Common sense," cried the King, "or these ears of mine have never heard it."

And he sent forth his herald Crispin to order that all spinning-wheels of whatever size, or age, should be destroyed, on penalty of death.

Because the people greatly loved the baby Princess, they gladly broke up and burned and disposed of every spinning-wheel in the land.

And Princess Rose grew up from a toddler to a little girl and from a little girl to a teenager.

With every year that passed, she became more beautiful, more kind and loving and more beloved by all the people.

By the time the Princess's sixteenth birthday came round, everyone had forgotten all about the wicked fairy's curse. The Princess had a wonderful birthday breakfast with so many presents that she lost count of them.

After breakfast, she said gaily: "I'm going to go round the palace from the cellar to the attic and thank everyone for the delightful presents and the marvellous birthday they've given me."

It was afternoon before the Princess had ended her tour of the castle. She was about to run downstairs when she noticed a queer little crooked staircase she did not remember having seen before.

"I wonder," she said to herself, "wherever this can lead to?"

She climbed the twisty flight and came to a closed door. There were cobwebs on the handle, but it turned easily at her touch and the door creaked open.

She found herself in a round, small room of crooked corners with a high painted ceiling. In the middle of the room stood something the Princess had never seen in her life. It was a spinning-wheel and an old woman was making the wheel sing as she spun.

The Princess was delighted.

"Please, please," she said, "May I try to make the wheel spin round?"

"Of course, dearie," replied the old woman. The Princess did not see the wicked gleam in her eye.

As soon as she touched the spinning-wheel, its spindle pricked her finger. The Princess dropped to the floor. All the colour drained from her cheeks, and she lay there as if dead.

In the same instant everyone in the castle fell asleep, from the King and Queen on their thrones to the kitchen maid who had been about to box the ears of the pantry boy. All fell asleep.

The old woman, who was, of course, the wicked fairy, uttered a shriek of laughter and flew out of the attic window on her broomstick.

She flew three times round the castle and as she did so a ring of wildly tangled briars sprang up. They encircled the castle in such thick confusion and with such sharp thorns that not even a mouse could have crept through.

Now it happened that early on the morning of the Princess's sixteenth birthday the royal herald had remembered that he had promised to allow his favourite niece to sit in a corner of the musician's gallery and watch the gay goings on. He slipped out of the palace and set off for the little girl, who lived in a village some miles away. But little Caroline was like most women and wasn't ready. By the time her mother had finished looping up her laces and tying up her hair, most of the morning had gone.

"Hurry up, Caroline, do," urged the herald.

Caroline hurried as fast as her fat little legs would let her, but they seemed fated not to reach the palace. They were just in sight of its towers and turrets, when, suddenly as a summer storm begins, they saw a tremendous hedge of briars spring up all round it.

And there the briars remained, in an unbreakable ring, for ninety-nine years, eleven months, three weeks and a day.

The herald was long since dead. His son was dead. His grandson was growing an old man. But the story of the bad fairy's curse had been passed down to him. He kept a calendar on which he ticked off the years, the months, the days and now the time was ripe. He sent out a proclamation in the King's name to offer half the kingdom to any prince who could break the spell.

Exactly one hundred years to the day after the ring of briars sprang up, Prince Rurik of Karelia took the sword of his fathers and drew it to hack his way through the briars. It was June and the briar hedge was as thickly strewn with white roses as the Milky Way with stars. The flowers called out to Rurik: "Spare us and we will help you."

The Prince sheathed his sword and the briar roses began to shed their petals so heavily as their branches parted, that they made a pathway for the Prince.

On entering the castle he found everyone sleeping. The pantry boy still had his arm raised to protect the ear the kitchen maid had been about to box a hundred years before. He went all through the palace and came at last to a narrow, twisty staircase. And there, in the turret room at the top, he saw the Princess fast asleep, her golden hair hanging down her back. Her lovely face was as marble-white as a statue. Kneeling, Prince Rurik kissed her on her lips.

At once her marble coldness became warm and loving and her eyes opened. They were as blue as Bavarian gentians. As the Prince gathered her into his arms, all the people in the palace woke up, the pantry boy in particular, when the kitchen maid boxed his ears!

And none of them knew that they had been asleep for a hundred years. When Rurik explained to the King and Queen what had happened, they needed a lot of convincing.

"Look," said the King, pointing to the window, "where is this hedge of briars you talk about?"

"It has disappeared with the breaking of the spell, Your Majesty," said Rurik. "But it has left proof behind. All round the palace is a ring which looks like midwinter snow— but it smells like all the roses that ever blew in June."

So it did, and the King was convinced.

"Prince," he cried, "I will give you as a reward half of my kingdom."

But the Princess cried: "Oh, Father, no, no, no, no, no. Give Rurik my hand in marriage instead. We fell in love the moment I opened my eyes."

"Ah well," said the King, "you shall have her."

"With my blessing," added the Queen.

"And in due course our son-in-law shall have not the half but the whole of the kingdom as well," they agreed.

"Not for this many a year," said the Prince and Princess. "Don't forget you've both got a hundred years of lost time to catch up with!"

Jack and the Beanstalk

After the death of her husband, a poor widow woman was left with a very small farm with which to support herself and her son Jack. All they had were two or three fields, half a dozen hens, two sheep and one cow.

"Now Jack," said the widow, "we can manage well enough if we work well. The sheep will provide wool from which I can make clothes for both of us. The hens will lay eggs, the cow will provide milk and we can grow vegetables in the kitchen garden."

"Yes, Mother," said Jack.

"Mind you, Jack, it will mean hard work."

"Of course, Mother," said Jack. "You do the work and I'll sympathize."

The widow sighed. This was no more than she had expected. The fact of the matter was that Jack was bone idle.

They managed well enough for a while. Then, one summer, drought struck the land. Cabbages, cauliflowers and carrots wilted and died in the kitchen garden. The hens all moulted and laid no more eggs. The grass withered in the fields and the sheep lost all their wool. Worst of all, Daisy, the cow gave no more milk. Her hide, once so sleek, was stretched over her body. Her ribs stuck out like those of an old umbrella blown inside out by the wind.

"Jack, my son," said the widow, "there's nothing for it now. You must take our cow to market and sell her for the best price you can get."

"Yes, Mother," replied Jack, "but it's a long way to market and I feel tired even before I start."

"Be off with you, you idle rascal," said his mother, "before I box your ears!"

So Jack set off for market, driving Daisy before him. On the way they came across a patch of wayside grass by a little stream. Daisy grazed on it all that afternoon and was given strength to reach the market before sundown.

A rich farmer, who sized up Jack for the fool he was, said: "Boy, I'll give you five beans for that cow. Do you know, boy, how many beans make five?"

"No sir," said Jack, "not being a scholar. But five beans seem to me to be a fair price for the cow."

The farmer counted out the five beans into Jack's hand and home the lad went.

When Jack's mother heard that he had sold Daisy for five beans she burst into tears, boxed his ears soundly and sent him to bed. Then she threw the five beans out of the kitchen window and went to bed to sob herself to sleep.

At sunrise next morning, Jack woke up and thought it was still the middle of the night. His bedroom was so dark he couldn't see his hand before his face. He made his way to the window and threw up the sash.

The beans his mother had thrown out had taken root in the kitchen garden. In the night they had grown together into an enormous beanstalk reaching up into the clouds.

Jack climbed out of the window and began to climb the beanstalk.

"Jack!" shouted his mother. "You'll break your neck! Come down this minute!"

Jack was already too high up to hear her. He climbed and climbed and climbed. Towards sunset he had reached the clouds and was at the top of the magic beanstalk.

Before him lay a gentle, beautiful country

of green fields and winding lanes. Not far away he saw a great white castle surrounded by a moat of sparkling water. The drawbridge was down, the castle door was wide open, so Jack crossed over and entered boldly.

He found himself in a vast hall. Before him was a wide corridor, ending in a closed door.

Jack marched briskly along and pushed as hard as he could against the closed door. It opened easily onto a large kitchen. The table was spread with good things to eat. Jack pulled himself up onto a chair and began to tuck in, for he was very hungry after his long climb.

He was just polishing off an enormous helping of currant pastry when he heard the sound of heavy footsteps approaching. A great voice roared:

"Fee, fi, fo, fum. I smell the blood of an Englishman."

The oven door was ajar, the fire out. Jack hid himself inside just in time. A red-headed giant strode into the room. The giant sat down at the table and began to grumble to himself.

"Must have been dreaming," he muttered. "Nobody here."

He pulled a bottle of wine across the table and, putting its neck to his lips, began to drink slowly. Before the bottle was quite empty, he put his head on his arms and went to sleep. His snores made the walls shake.

Jack crept out of the oven. At the giant's belt hung two huge moneybags. Standing on a kitchen stool, Jack unhooked first one and then the other moneybag from the giant's belt. He slung both of them over his shoulder and off he went.

When he reached the outer door of the castle, he dropped one of the moneybags. It made a great sound of jingling and jangling which echoed through the corridor. Jack heard the giant wake up with a roar. He grabbed the fallen moneybag and began to run, staggering, to the top of the beanstalk. As he started to climb down, the ground shook under the pounding feet of the giant.

Down, down, down Jack climbed, through the clouds and down towards the earth far below. He could see his mother's cottage, but looking up he could also see the huge booted feet of the giant.

With his heart in his mouth, Jack began to scramble down even faster.

"Mother," he yelled. "Fetch the axe from the woodshed!"

His mother ran to do so.

Jack dropped first one and then the other moneybag to the foot of the beanstalk and slid the last forty feet to the ground. Then he picked up the axe and began to hack away like fury at the trunk of the stalk.

"My gold! My gold!" roared the giant.

"Oh, I'll spit you and roast you, I'll boil you and baste you when I lay hands on you. I'll have you for breakfast with fried button mushrooms. Fee, fo, fi . . ."

"Fum," shouted Jack and gave the beanstalk a last whack with his axe.

The beanstalk shuddered and crashed, just missing the roof of the cottage. The red-haired giant fell with a thud which shook the whole garden like an earthquake. Then he lay still, with his arms outspread. He had broken his neck.

And all over the giant, the fallen beanstalk and the kitchen garden, lay scattered the golden coins from the moneybags.

"There, Mother," said Jack. "Hold out your apron. I may not know how many beans make five, but you can count. Let's see how many gold pieces it takes to fill one apron."

It took five apronfuls to fill one of the widow's clothes baskets and five clothes baskets to fill the woodshed.

The next day Jack went back to the market, sought out the farmer who had bought Daisy for five beans and paid him fifty gold pieces to buy her back again.

"Moo-oo," said Daisy, "I can't eat nasty gold. It's no use to me."

"Never mind," said Jack. "I'll buy you stacks and stacks of sweet clover hay and you can chew the cud happily for the rest of your life."

The funny thing was that idle Jack, from that day on, became industrious John and added farm to farm until he was the richest landowner for miles around.

The best thing was that his hard-working mother never did another hand's turn, but spent all day like a fine lady, doing just what she wanted to; and to the end of their days neither of them ever bothered again about how many beans made five.

The Frog Prince

A certain King Helmut and his lovely wife Queen Helga had an only child, Princess Magda.

From the day of her birth the King loved his daughter so much that by the time she was three she could twist him round her little finger. And well the child knew it. The Queen loved her little daughter, too, but Magda knew to half an inch how far she dared go with her mother and was careful never to venture any farther. Except now and then, of course, when her natural sense of mischief provoked her.

On such occasions Queen Helga used to say: "Now, Magda. Do as you're told, or I shall smack you. Try to behave properly."

When this happened, King Helmut would push his crown back from his head and remark: "My dear, just remembered. Must see the Prime Minister. State business." And he would hurry out of the room while the Queen rolled her sleeves up.

When the King came back, he would find that Princess Magda was as good as the little girl who had a little curl right in the middle of her forehead. And she would stay that way for sometimes as long as a week.

As Princess Magda grew up into a more and more beautiful girl, she grew, if possible even more mischievous.

On the day of her sixteenth birthday her favourite uncle, the Count of Luxembourg, gave her a very pretty thing indeed. It was a ball as light as thistledown, covered with gold leaf which made it glitter in the sun.

It took the Princess's fancy. She ran out into the walled rose garden and began to invent games she could play with it. She bounced it two hundred and three times on the velvet-smooth lawn. Then she began to throw it in the air and catch it. When she tired of that, she shut her eyes, threw it in the air again and tried to catch it without opening her eyes.

Splash! When Princess Magda opened her eyes she saw the pretty golden ball floating on the surface of the lily pool. A fish rose from the water and took a bite at it so that it sank and lay glistening among the lily roots.

The Princess, who had been spoilt all her life, began to weep fretfully because she wanted something she could not have.

Just then a large fat frog swam up from the crystal depths and sat on the rim of the lily pool.

"Princess," he croaked, "What will you give me if I dive down and bring you back your pretty plaything?"

"Anything, anything," cried Princess Magda.

"Very well. I'll rescue your golden ball if you will let me sit at the table with you and sleep at night on your pillow."

"Bring me back my pretty plaything and I will do anything you ask."

"Promise," said the frog.

"Promise. A princess's word."

The frog dived down and in a moment surfaced with the golden ball clasped in his front claws.

Without even saying "thank you" the Princess ran indoors.

The frog hopped after her.

"Send that ugly creature away," the Princess told one of the footmen.

Now Queen Helga happened to be in the hall, so the frog told her the story of Princess Magda's promise.

"Is it true?" asked the Queen.

"Yes," said Magda sulkily.

"Promises must never, never be broken," said the Queen. "Especially not promises made by royals."

The Princess pouted. But the frog hopped first onto a chair and then onto the table.

"I hate you," said Magda.

"A promise is a promise," said the Queen,

warningly.

"Oh, very well. What do you eat, you ugly thing? Worms, I suppose."

"No, dear Princess. I'll nibble a piece of cake, taste a bit of your bread and honey and drink a little of your China tea."

Mortified, the Princess fed the frog.

The same thing happened at supper.

"I'm off to bed early," the Princess said.

"So am I," croaked the frog.

"You're not to come in my room," said the Princess.

"A promise . . ." began the Queen.

"Oh, very well," snapped the Princess.

The frog hopped after her, step by step, and followed her to her bedroom door.

"Go away," said the Princess, "you little horror, you."

The Queen's voice floated up the stairway.

"A promise is a promise. Especially one given by a royal."

"Oh, come on," said the Princess. The frog hopped after her and slammed the door. When the Princess had put on her lace nightie, she said her prayers and got into bed.

"As for you," she said, "You can go and sleep in that corner over there. And I hope you have nightmares."

The frog croaked sadly.

"Must I croak all night, Princess? I can you know. I have a very deep voice."

And he began to croak so loudly that the Queen heard him—indeed the whole palace heard him.

"Oh come here and shut up," said the Princess.

The frog stopped croaking and jumped in

one big jump onto the Princess's pillow. There he slept all night, very soundly. Not so Princess Magda. She could not snatch a wink for weeping with rage and spite.

When the rising sun shone, the frog yawned and stretched himself.

"What a very pleasant, refreshing slumber," he said. "I shall look forward to many, many more, Princess."

"Oh, no!" she pleaded. "I couldn't stand another night like that."

"Then I'll make a bargain with you," said the frog. "Kiss me full on the mouth and I'll never torment you again."

The Princess shut her eyes as tight as tight could be and kissed the frog.

She had dreaded the touch of his mouth but to her great surprise she found herself being delightfully kissed by warm, en-thusiastic lips. She opened her eyes—and found herself in the arms of a tall, dark, handsome young man.

"Princess," he explained. "My name is Prince Conrad of Ruraliese. When I was christened, my parents forgot to invite my fairy godmother, but she turned up in a vile temper and changed me into a frog. Then she told me that I would remain a frog until a royal princess let me sit at table and share her meals and afterwards allowed me to sleep on her pillow. And if she kissed me full on the mouth," Conrad added, "the spell would be broken and I would become my true self again. Oh, Princess Magda, I love you, I love you. Will you marry me?"

"No," said Princess Magda.

But Conrad knew by the look in her eyes that she meant "yes". And she did.

The Golden Goose

There was once a woodcutter who had three sons. The two older boys were good and clever, but their parents and everyone else agreed that the youngest, Stefan, was a fool.

One day the father of the family fell ill.

"Never mind, Father," said Albert, the eldest son. "I'll go into the forest and cut wood. You've taught me to use an axe."

"Good boy," said the father.

"Mother, bake him a cake and give him a bottle of home-made lemonade."

So mother baked a big gingerbread cake, gave him a bottle of home-made lemonade and off Albert went.

On his way, he met a little grey man, who said: "Please, I'm hungry and thirsty. Give me a piece of that gingerbread cake and a little drink of lemonade."

"Certainly not," said Albert. "How do you think I can cut down trees all day without plenty to eat and drink?"

He marched on, found a tall tree and began to swing his axe. His axe struck once, twice and then hit his arm, cutting it badly. Albert went home.

"I can't cut any more wood," he said.

Next morning, Joseph, the second son said: "I'll go and cut wood."

"Good lad," said his father.

"Mother, bake him a plum cake and give him a bottle of home-made wine."

"Of course I will," said mother.

So Joseph set off with the plum cake and the home-made wine.

Soon he met the little grey man who said: "I'm hungry and thirsty. Please give me a small slice of that beautiful plum cake and a sip of home-made wine."

"Be off," said Joseph. "I've got to eat and drink to keep up my health and strength."

He marched on and soon began to swing his axe at the trunk of a beech. Once he struck, twice—and then the axe slipped and cut his leg. Joseph went home.

"I can't work any more," he said.

Next morning the youngest son, Stefan, said: "I know I'm not very good at cutting trees. But dear parents, I'll have a go."

"You?" said father. "You wouldn't know how to swing the axe properly. But just to teach you not to be conceited, off you go. Mother, bake him a cake and give him something to drink."

Stefan's mother baked him a nasty little dough cake with a currant or two in it and filled a bottle with water. Off Stefan went.

Stefan hadn't gone far before he met the little grey man who said: "I'm hungry and oh, I am thirsty. Please give me a piece of cake and a drink of water."

"Of course I will," said Stefan. He unwrapped the nasty little dough cake and was amazed to find that it was a huge chocolate-cake stuffed with cream. The bottle of water when it was poured out foamed with the creamiest ginger beer.

"Thank you," said the little grey man. "Yum. Now take your axe and cut down this oak tree. At the roots you'll find something good."

Stefan began to cut down the oak. When it crashed, he found at its roots a golden goose, with every feather gleaming in the sunlight. Stefan tucked it under his arm and went on his way, feeling very pleased with himself.

The forest paths which Stefan knew so well now seemed somehow different. Presently he came to a village he had never seen before. There was an inn and, as light was falling fast, Stefan decided he'd better spend the night there. The landlord gave one look at the golden goose under Stefan's arm and made him very welcome. He was given a splendid supper and the best bedroom.

Now the landlord had three attractive daughters. Each of them had seen the golden goose, and each of them had an idea about it. About midnight the eldest girl crept into Stefan's room and tried to pluck a golden feather from the goose. As soon as her fingers touched the feather they stuck as though caught in the strongest glue.

At one in the morning the second daughter crept into the room.

"So you thought you could steal a march on me," she whispered, seeing her sister stuck fast to the goose. She too, tried to pluck a golden feather and her fingers also stuck hard. At two in the morning the youngest daughter crept in. She tried to pull her two sisters away. As soon as she touched one of them her fingers stuck.

In the morning, Stefan woke up.

"Good gracious," he said. "This is no place for me."

He tucked the goose under his arm and set off. The three sisters had to follow him. Soon the little procession passed a farmer's wife. She, too, tried to pluck a golden feather, and she too was trapped. In every village they passed through young women and old women, boys and men tried to grab a feather from the golden goose. Old and young, ploughboys, goose-girls, mayors in scarlet robes, lawyers with quill pens dripping ink over their collars, a dairy-maid, a duchess and a parson, a bride and bridegroom and a clown from a travelling circus, all tried to pluck a feather from the golden goose and each and every one of them stuck fast and was forced to follow Stefan. But Stefan took no notice of any of them. He just went marching on with the goose tucked under his arm.

At about four o'clock one afternoon he came to a big city. It was the capital of the country and all the town turned out to greet the procession.

Now it so happened that the Princess Amanda was of a very sad and serious disposition. Nothing had ever made her smile since she was born. This troubled the King and Queen greatly and it was well known in all that country that whoever made Princess Amanda laugh for the first time could have her royal hand in marriage.

Clowns and town councillors, princes and pastrycooks, beggars and even bandits had tried to get a smile from her—and with it her hand. But all in vain. Princess Amanda was so sad that she sighed on even the most golden of summer days and in winter she cried practically all day long.

That day, when Stefan entered the town with his golden goose and all the raggle-taggle people who were forced to march with it, the King's jester was busy trying to make the Princess smile. She was sitting on her hands in a bay window overlooking the market square and her maids of honour were all encouraging the jester to raise even the faintest smile on her lips.

Now it happened that news had just reached the Bavarian court. In those days, of course, there was no radio, no television, not even a newspaper, so news was scarce and highly interesting, whatever it happened to be.

"Your Royal Highness," said the jester, shaking the silver bells on his cap, "there seems to have been a great naval battle between the French and the English at the sea port of Suys."

"Oh dear," said the Princess, her eyes beginning to fill with tears at the thought of it.

The jester, whose dress was one half red and the other half yellow, like the pied piper of Hamelin, danced a cheerful step or two and tried again.

"The English won a splendid victory. They sank so many ships and captured so many others that nobody dared give the bad news to the King of France for more than a week. Then the King's jester, a cousin of mine, had the nerve to tell him. 'Your Majesty,' he said, 'We French have proved our superiority to the English sailors. Our brave French sailors all jumped into the sea, but the cowardly English dared not follow them.'"

All the maids of honour clapped their hands and tittered.

"Oh dear, the poor, poor French sailors,"

said the Princess, and burst into tears.

"What can you do with a girl like her?" the jester asked. "Can't see a joke no matter how funny it is."

At that moment Stefan and his strange followers came in sight as they crossed the market square. The three sisters who had tried to steal a feather from the golden goose were each writhing about trying to get their hands free of the goose's feathers. Woodcutters, clowns, a second parson, a whole troop of beggars, a miller and three more lawyers had all joined the long train, and were all dragged along behind the goose. Every single person danced and capered and kicked his heels; they looked like so many puppets, jerked by invisible strings, as they tried their best to free themselves.

A strange sound came from the window: a sound never heard in the palace before. Princess Amanda was laughing.

All the maids of honour joined in. The jester rolled on the floor holding his sides. And Princess Amanda laughed and laughed and laughed until tears of mirth rolled down her cheeks. She was making up for years and years with never a smile and she sounded like it. In rushed the King, in ran the Queen and all the courtiers. They were all seized with irresistible fits of laughter. Only the court chamberlain, who was too short and fat to look through the window, but understood that someone in the market square had made the Princess laugh, ran as fast as his fat little legs could carry him and brought Stefan into the palace. As soon as he put down the golden goose to bow to the King and Queen, all the prisoners of the goose were released from the magic spell and ran helter skelter out of the palace and away to their homes.

Need I add that although Stefan was dressed half in rags he was so gay and handsome that the Princess was only too happy to marry him? They lived happily ever after and ever after the golden goose had a place of honour at court and became the favourite pet of the children who were later born to the happy pair.

The Clever Cook

A rich merchant called Herman Schmidt was anxious to make a good impression on the local mayor and he asked him to dinner. The mayor agreed and it was soon settled: he would come to the merchant's house on the evening of the following Friday.

Now Herman had a clever cook whose name was Margaret. On her advice it was agreed that a simple but very good dinner should be prepared: two plump roasting chickens and a rich sherry trifle.

Friday came and the merchant set off early in the morning on a matter of business.

"I'll be back this evening just before six o'clock," he said. "Mind you have everything ready."

Now Margaret, though she was a wonderful cook, was fat, greedy and lazy. As she made the fire she grumbled to her cat, Truffles.

"What thanks will I get from my master, Cat?" she asked. "Nothing. I've got to slave all day just to make a meal for the master and one guest. As much trouble as cooking for twelve."

"Miau," said the cat. "Mee-ilk."

"You shall have some of the cream for the trifle," said Margaret. She poured out a saucer of cream, drank half of it herself and gave the rest to Truffles. Then Margaret put the two chickens in a big roasting-tin in the oven.

She sat and stared at the fire. This made her feel thirsty, so she drank most of the cooking sherry.

"Fire's nice and hot, Truffles," she said. "Makes me hungry." She nibbled some of the sponge cake for the trifle. Then she drank the rest of the cooking sherry and went into the cellar for another bottle. When she returned to the kitchen she sniffed.

"I think one of the chickens is burning, Truffles." She opened the oven door. The wing tip of one chicken was very slightly singed.

"Won't do for the master's guest, Truffles," she muttered, and she cut off the wing, shut

the oven and began to eat the wing in her fingers. When she had nearly finished it, she gave the rest to Truffles. Then she had another look in the oven.

"That chicken looks lopsided, Cat," she said. "Master might notice. Tell you what, Cat. I'll cut the other wing off and then it will look nice and even."

The cook and the cat finished off the other wing. Time was passing. The cook began to prepare the trifle. She lined a big glass dish with sponge cake, spread with raspberry jam. As the cat didn't like raspberry jam, the cook ate half the jarful herself. She whipped the cream and looked into the oven again. The chicken without wings was done to a turn and smelt so appetizing that the cook and the cat finished it off between them.

Half an hour later the cook decided that the second, plump and larger chicken was beginning to burn. Indeed, one of its legs was slightly singed and rather brown.

"We'll cut it off, Cat," said Margaret. "Master's very particular about meals being cooked to perfection."

She cut off the leg, ate threequarters of it and gave Truffles the rest.

Another half hour passed. Margaret had another look in the oven.

"Doing nicely, Cat," she said. "But this chicken looks even more lopsided than the first one did. I'll trim it." She cut off the second leg, which went the same way as the first.

"Nibbling," said Margaret, "makes me thirsty." She gave the cat some more cream and drank most of the rest of the second bottle of cooking sherry, leaving just a teaspoon or two for the trifle. Then she had another look in the oven.

"Oh," said Margaret. "It's done to a turn. But where's the master? Where's his guest, the mayor?"

"Miaua?" said Truffles, mistaking the word mayor for more.

"How right you are," said Margaret. She put the second chicken on a big plate and she and the cat finished it off between them.

Margaret was just licking her fingers in a satisfied sort of way when she heard the distant sound of hoofbeats.

"Miaua," said Truffles.

"Exactly," said Margaret. "The Master."

As the sound of galloping hooves came nearer, Truffles ran up the kitchen curtain and hid himself on top of the pelmet.

"Meee—ee—a—ow," he said. "Now you're for it, Margaret."

The merchant threw himself off his horse, stabled it, sponged it down, put some oats in the manger, and came stamping into the kitchen.

"Ha," he said, sniffing appreciatively. "What a delicious, warm, appetizing smell is coming from that oven of yours, Margaret. It's nearly six o'clock. The mayor is a man who believes that punctuality is the politeness of princes. Is the meal nearly ready?"

"Not quite, sir," said Margaret. "I've made the trifle. It's under this damp cloth. The chickens are done to a turn. Truffles the cat would give one of his ears to have a go at them. I'll dish them up as soon as your guest arrives."

"Capital, capital," said the merchant, rubbing his hands. "Ah, what a blessing it is to have a really splendid cook like you, Margaret to look after me and my guest. Give me the carving knife. I'll sharpen it on the back doorstep."

"Certainly, sir," said the cook and handed to her master a huge, bone-handled carving knife. Herman went out into the yard and began to sharpen the carving knife on the back doorstep.

Just as the clock struck six, Margaret heard a knock at the front door. There stood the mayor, hat in hand, a smile of expectation on his face.

Margaret threw up her hands and gave a small shriek.

"Oh Mr. Mayor, sir," she said, "thank heavens I've managed to intercept you in the nick of time. My master has gone clean out of his mind. He swears he'll cut off first your ears and then your head. Listen. Can you hear him? He's sharpening the carving knife on the back doorstep at this minute."

The mayor turned paler than an under-ripe cheese, turned on his heels and began to run for his life.

"That's got rid of him, Truffles," said the cook as she re-entered the kitchen. "Now for my master." She ran to the back doorstep.

"Master, Master," she gasped. "Your guest the mayor has taken leave of his senses. He came rushing into the house, snatched the two chickens off this dish and rushed off with both of them shouting that you had stolen them from the town cryer and he'll have the law on you."

The merchant turned as purple at this as the mayor had turned pale.

"Thanks for the warning, Margaret," he cried. "Those idiots on the town council will believe every word he says about anything. They always do. He'll blacken my good name and ruin me unless I can stop him in time."

Out of the front-door he rushed and, running down the road, he began to yell and bawl at the mayor.

"Stop. Come back. I want you."

There was a bright moon by this time, and, looking over his shoulder, the mayor could see the merchant pounding after him, the carving knife in his hand flashing dreadfully in the moonlight. He put on a terrific burst of speed. Aroused by the merchant's shouts and the mayor's yells of terror, half the town turned out to see what was going on. The watch brought their lanterns and blunderbusses. All the town dogs started to bark. The mayor ran clean through the town with the merchant at his heels and the watch, the townsfolk and the dogs, all trailing behind.

"There, Truffles," cried Margaret. "Now you and I can sit down comfortably and finish the trifle and the rest of the cooking sherry between us."

Cinderella

Once upon a time there were two ugly sisters named Niminy and Piminy who had a good deal of money which they had inherited from their parents. They lived in a fine house and were supposed to look after their little sister, Cinderella.

Now Cinderella was a beautiful and loving child, so different from her ugly sisters that both of them were jealous of her. Out of sheer spite, therefore, they made Cinderella's life as much of a misery as they could.

"Where's your sense of gratitude, Cinderella?" said Niminy. "Piminy and I do everything for you. We give you a roof over your head, food to eat and warmth and shelter. It's up to you, wretched child, to show your gratitude."

"That's right," said Piminy. "Gratitude! You don't know the meaning of the word. In return for our kindness you must rise early and light the kitchen fire. Then you must make us our breakfast and bring it to us in bed."

"After which," added Niminy, "you must wash and scrub and dust and polish and keep the fire burning and have our lunch ready for us when we choose to get up."

"I'll try," said Cinderella. "I'll do my best."

But her best never satisfied her cruel sisters. While they dressed in fine clothes of silk and satin, poor Cinderella only had one new dress a year and it soon became tattered and torn with all the work she did.

It happened that not far away from where the three sisters lived was the castle of Prince Florizel, the youngest and most handsome of all the princes in Europe. One day he decided to give a ball, and sent out invitations, which included one to the three sisters.

Now Niminy and Piminy were as vain as they were ugly. They began to make plans.

"This is our great chance," said Niminy. "Who knows, the Prince may fall in love with me and ask me to marry him."

"You mean," argued Piminy, "he'll fall in love with me."

"If he does," said Niminy, "I'll scratch your eyes out."

"And I'll scratch yours out if he falls in love with you," replied the other.

"One thing's certain—Cinderella shan't go to the ball."

"That she shan't. As though the Prince would fall in love with an ugly little thing like her." They both roared with laughter.

So the two ugly sisters dressed themselves in silks and satins and went off in a hired coach to the castle.

"Oh dear," sighed Cinderella. "How I should have loved to have gone, too. But how could I? I have nothing to wear but my one torn and tattered dress. Ah, well. I'll sit by the fire and hope my two sisters will enjoy themselves."

Presently, the only friends she had, eight little mice, crept out of their hole and joined the warmth of the fireside circle.

"Hello, darlings," said Cinderella. "Nice to see you. But I can't sit here by the fire just talking to you. I ought to set about making a pumpkin pie while the oven's hot."

The fire suddenly leaped up. Its dancing flames lit the kitchen—and then the gold of the firelight changed to dazzling silver.

"Cinderella," said a sweet and thrilling voice, "I am your fairy godmother. You *shall* go to the ball. You've had enough sorrow lately."

She waved her fairy wand. At once, Cinderella's rags were changed into a lovely long gown of grass green. The pumpkin became a coach and the eight mice were turned into fine white horses. Last of all, the fairy godmother gave Cinderella a pair of glass shoes to dance in.

"Size two," she said. "You have the smallest and loveliest feet in all Floristan. Now be off and enjoy yourself. There's only one condition. You must return and

sit among the cinders again before the clock strikes midnight."

"Oh, I will, I will, dearest of fairy godmothers," she promised.

The instant Prince Florizel set eyes on Cinderella, he fell in love with her. In his arms she seemed to drift as in a dream.

The night passed swiftly.

"It's like dancing with about two ounces of thistledown," said the Prince. "I love you, Cinderella. Will you . . ."

Before he could finish his proposal, the palace clock struck. It was midnight already!

Cinderella remembered the fairy godmother's warning just in time. She turned and fled from the palace and in her haste she lost one of her glass dancing shoes. Even as she was running away across the great lawn, her clothes turned back to her normal ragged ones; as she reached the gate two small grey mice ran squeaking away from a large pumpkin lying abandoned at the side of the road.

When the two ugly sisters returned from the ball, they were in very bad tempers. They had not, of course, recognized their sister, looking like a princess as she danced with Prince Florizel. But as he had not asked either of them to dance, they were sour with disappointment.

Meanwhile, Prince Florizel was in the depths of misery himself. He could neither eat nor drink nor sleep for thinking about the lovely girl who had come from nowhere to dance with him and capture his heart. The only thing he had to help him to find her was the glass dancing shoe.

As he held the shoe in his hand, he had a sudden inspiration. He sent for his herald and ordered him to seek and find the girl whose foot fitted the shoe.

The herald tried the shoe on foot after foot, but found none that fitted. At last he arrived at the house where the ugly sisters lived.

"I think my foot can squeeze into this shoe," said Niminy. "I take a size seven, but eights are so comfortable that I always wear nines. This looks just right."

"You're lucky," replied Piminy. "I take a size eight, but nines are so comfortable that I always wear tens."

"Do not trouble," said the herald, "to try to put even your toes into this shoe."

Then he noticed Cinderella, in her rags and tatters, sitting among the cinders and trying to make the fire burn by working a pair of bellows.

"Will you try on this glass dancing shoe?" he asked.

"No use asking her," snapped Niminy.

"Can't you see her dress is all tattered and torn?"

"You must be out of your mind," added Piminy. "A scruffy little thing like Cinderella would not even have been allowed in the castle kitchen to help in washing up the dishes!"

"Ladies," said the herald, "I'm not interested in whether her dress is in tatters or in her ability to wash dishes. All I want to know is whether or not her foot fits the shoe."

He knelt among the cinders, and, when Cinderella put out her foot, the glass shoe fitted it more closely than a glove.

Still in her rags, Cinderella was driven straight to the castle in the Prince's own coach, drawn by the royal cream horses, with outriders and trumpeters to clear the way. All the people came flocking to admire and cheer. The minute the royal coach crossed the drawbridge, Prince Florizel rushed to meet it.

"My love, my darling!" he cried. "I have found you again. How soon can you marry me?"

The wedding of Prince Florizel and his lovely bride is still talked about in Floristan, the land of flowers. And as the wedding bells promised, the Prince and his Princess lived happily ever after.

Even to this day those who were lucky enough to be guests at the wedding keep a piece of the wedding cake. As for the ugly sisters, I'm not sorry to tell you that they lived unhappily ever after.

The Return of Spring

Legend has it that Demeter, the corn goddess, had an only child, a daughter named Persephone. Gay, joyous and completely carefree, Persephone loved to wander in the fields and woods, plucking flowers and spreading happiness all around her.

But as Persephone gradually grew into a young woman, Demeter began to be uneasy about her.

"My darling," she said one day, "the world isn't the safe and innocent place you think it is. There are bad people about who may do you some harm."

"Oh, please don't be anxious, Mother," replied Persephone. "Everybody loves me."

"That's what you think," said Demeter. "You haven't my experience of the world. Listen to me, my darling. You may continue to wander the fields and woods, but mind you are always home before nightfall. And keep away from the Black River and the Wood of Dreams when twilight comes."

"Oh, I will, I will, if you insist," said Persephone.

But the very next afternoon Persephone completely forgot her promise. When the golden light began to fade into dusk, she strayed closer to the Wood of Dreams, searching for the fairest of all flowers, moly, which sometimes grows on the bank of the Black River.

She was just kneeling to pick a stalk of this when a low rumble, like thunder, caused her to spring to her feet. A quarter of a mile away, the side of a small hill split open and out rushed a black chariot, drawn by a pair of coal-black horses at full gallop. Driving them was a charioteer, blacker than midnight, whose eyes blazed more brilliantly than the diamonds in his jewel-studded crown. Persephone recognized him at once. He was the King of the Underworld.

The black horses swept the chariot toward her. The charioteer leaned sideways and snatched the terrified Persephone into his arms. The horses stretched their necks, their manes flying, and galloped back towards the gaping hole in the hillside. Persephone looked wildly about her. She saw the fields, the wood and the fading golden day—then the black tunnel swallowed horses, charioteer and the girl herself into absolute darkness.

Now it happened that some nearby children had witnessed the scene and they ran at once to tell Demeter. The corn goddess did not hesitate. She dressed in her most golden robe, brushed her long, shining hair and went straight to the court of Zeus the Thunderer, father of gods and men, on Mount Olympus.

Sobbing, she told her story.

"I demand my right as a goddess," she said. "Order the King of the Underworld to return my child to the light of day."

Zeus stroked his beard.

"The King of Hades is rich and powerful," he said. "He owns all the gold and silver in the earth, the emeralds and rubies and diamonds. Nevertheless, I, Zeus, can command him and he must obey. Provided that Persephone, your daughter, has not accepted from him in the underworld any food whatsoever."

Far down in the depths of the earth, Hades, King of the Underworld had prepared a magnificent banquet for his prisoner. One

after another, servants passed before her, each carrying a golden dish of superbly prepared food. There were great joints of meat, delicate vegetables, and cheeses of all shapes and sizes. Each servant paused in front of Persephone, persuading her to try—just to taste—even a morsel of his dish. And each time Persephone shook her lovely, sad head, and turned away. Last of all came a servant carrying a dish piled high with fruits from all over the world: with apples and oranges, plums, grapes, pears, peaches, mangoes—with every kind of fruit you can imagine. Balanced right on the very pinnacle was a ripe, juicy pomegranate.

By this time, Persephone was feeling both hungry and thirsty. Only her stubborn will not to accept anything from her captors had prevented her from eating before: now the sight of the pomegranate was too much. Half reluctantly she reached out her hand and raised it to her lips.

As she swallowed the first mouthful, a great, shuddering sigh seemed to shake the underground palace, and Hades spoke, his voice reverberating and echoing right up to the court of the gods on Olympus.

"Father of gods and men," he said, "Persephone has eaten six seeds of a pomegranate. And for each of the seeds she has eaten she must stay in the underworld for a month."

"I acknowledge," replied Zeus, "that these seeds are magic. And even the gods cannot break the spells of magic. Therefore, Persephone must remain in the underworld for six months of the year. At the end of that time, you must return her to the upper world. I have spoken."

For six months Demeter waited in mourning. The flowers died; the trees lost their leaves; frost and snow covered the land. Then, when the six months had passed, she put on a robe of shimmering, silver-green, which billowed about her like a field of barley smoothed by the hands of the wind. She went to the mouth of the underworld and demanded the return of Persephone.

As her voice echoed through Hades,

Cerberus, the three-headed dog who guards the entrance, rushed out of his kennel and began to howl and whine.

"Quiet!" commanded Demeter. "A mother's love will face and overcome the gates of hell itself. Return my daughter."

The King of the Underworld heard, scowling.

"Persephone," he said, "I love you. Stay with me and I will give you all the riches of the earth. You shall be the Queen of the Underworld and reign over my heart for ever."

"Persephone, don't listen to him," called Demeter. "One glimpse of the gold of the sun is worth all the jewels of the underworld."

The King tried to hold Persephone's wrists.

"Let me go!" she cried, struggling free.

"If you keep your part of the bargain, I'll keep mine. But now I must return to the upper world which has been grey and cold and miserable without me."

She dressed in a gown of new green silk, woven from the tears and laughter of an April day, and ran and ran. Three-headed Cerberus wagged his three tails and his three tongues licked her hands in farewell. Out of the dark mouth of Hades she sped and went dancing over the grass, her sandalled feet lightly brushing the dew, making it glitter in the early sunshine.

Wherever she touched the earth, king-cups and violets, daisies and celandines sprang up. The daffodils blew their golden trumpets to greet her. Swallows and swifts skimmed around her and all the birds sang jubilantly because spring had returned.

And the hearts of all men rejoiced with Demeter to know that the corn would grow again.

As for the King of the Underworld, in his dark kingdom, he also held a small glow of happiness in his heart. For he knew that when the harvest had been safely gathered in, Persephone would return to him to gladden and make endurable the long, dreary, winter, even in Hades.

Aladdin and the Wonderful Lamp

In the Lotus City of Pekin there lived a poor woman, the Widow Twankey, who supported herself and her son Aladdin by taking in washing. Young, gay and lean—for he often went hungry—Aladdin was an adventurous boy. One day he did what no other boy had ever dared to do. He climbed over the wall of the Jade Button Mandarin's palace.

In the Garden of Jasmine Blossoms he found the most beautiful girl he had ever seen. She was the mandarin's daughter, the Princess So-Shi. So-Shi was so high-born that no other children were allowed to play with her. Imagine how delighted she was when Aladdin taught her how to play hide-and-seek. All afternoon they played, finding new and better places to hide all the time. She was hiding behind a yellow rose bush when her father came angrily into the garden and at once ordered Aladdin to go home; and not to return upon pain of death.

Weeping, Aladdin gave Princess So-Shi a jasmine flower.

"Remember me by this, for ever," said Aladdin.

The Princess, too upset to speak, nodded.

Now there lived in the Lotus City a magician whose name was Abanazar. One day, a merchant sold him for a trifling sum a dull old ring. Abanazar did not think he would be able to sell the ring for much money, but something about it appealed to him, and he slipped it on his finger and forgot it. Later that day, he twisted it idly round his finger—a nervous habit rather like biting his nails! He was extremely startled when suddenly a spirit appeared, bowed and said:

"I am the Slave of the Ring. What are your commands, Master?"

"Give me power. Absolute power," said Abanazar at once.

"Only the Genie of the Lamp can do that, Master. I can make a plum tree grow from nowhere, or cherry blossoms float from the air instead of snow in winter . . ."

"Bah," snarled Abanazar. "Where can I find the Wonderful Lamp?"

"It's in the Cave of all Caves, in the Mountains of the Roof of the World, Master."

"Take me there instantly."

"I can do that, Master. But it wouldn't help. The cave has been sealed for ten thousand years by a moss-grown rock. You are far too fat to squeeze through the narrow tunnel. Only a lean, active boy could do that."

Now Abanazar had seen just such a lean, active boy running about the market place: the son of the Widow Twankey. After making discreet enquiries, he soon discovered who Aladdin was and the next evening he called at the tumble-down house where the boy and his mother lived.

Abanazar pretended to be the boy's long-lost rich uncle. With gifts of spinning tops and fighting kites he soon won the boy's affection. Then he offered to take Aladdin round the world to improve his education. The widow wept, but Abanazar's gift of a purse of gold comforted her a little and she allowed Aladdin to set out.

Many and marvellous adventures befell Aladdin before, nine months later, the two climbed above the snow-line and found the Cave of all Caves in the Mountains of the Roof of the World.

"I'm cold. I'm miserable. I want to go home," said Aladdin.

"Nonsense, boy." Abanazar rolled the stone from the mouth of the cave. Lifeless air that had been bottled up for ten thousand years made the narrow, midnight-black

tunnel a place of terror to Aladdin.

"Down," cried Abanazar in a cold, sinister voice. And he took his magic ring and thrust it onto Aladdin's forefinger. More frightened of this strange, new, terrible uncle than he was of the dreadful tunnel, Aladdin wriggled his way into the darkness of the cave. In a moment he cried out in amazement and joy.

"What can you see, boy?" called Abanazar.

"Jewels, uncle. Marvellous, glittering diamonds, pearls and rubies. Baskets and baskets of them."

"Baubles, boy. Toys for foolish girls. Can you see a lamp? The lamp of power, absolute power."

"There is an old, dull-looking lamp on a high stone shelf, uncle. Not worth the smallest of these fabulous jewels."

"Bring me the lamp," roared Abanazar.

Aladdin climbed to the high shelf and grasped the handle of the lamp. As he did so, he heard a voice—clear, cold and very far away:

"Seek not to grasp the mightiest power on earth. To hold it brings loneliness and sorrow beyond measure. Human, beware!"

"Bring me the lamp," roared Abanazar.

"No," cried Aladdin.

With a great curse, Abanazar rolled back the stone that sealed the cave. Instantly, the shimmering, glimmering light from the baskets of jewels vanished.

Terrified, alone in darkness, Aladdin threw himself, trembling to the floor. He clasped his hands together in terror. As he did so he felt the ring on his left finger, and twisted it.

Instantly all the jewel lights blazed out again. A small spirit stood before the boy.

"I am the Slave of the Ring. Command me and I obey."

Aladdin blinked.

"I suppose," said the genie "you want absolute power?"

"No," said Aladdin. "I'm hungry. I'm thirsty. I'd give anything for some nice, juicy plums."

"Instantly," said the slave. A plum tree

shot up in the middle of the jewelled baskets. Its branches were loaded with huge plums.

Aladdin ate until he was quite full.

"Now," he cried, "take me back to our dear little cottage in the Lotus City."

"Who, me?" asked the slave. "Couldn't. Only the Genie of the Lamp could do that. Just rub the lamp and he'll appear. Wait a minute. Let me get back into my ring."

He disappeared and Aladdin rubbed the lamp. A huge column of green smoke shot up to the roof of the Cave of Caves, became solid and was the Genie of the Lamp.

"Master, what are your commands?" he asked. "Speak—and I obey."

Aladdin remembered the warning voice which he had heard when he first touched the handle of the lamp.

"I don't want power and loneliness," he said. "I'd like you to change mother's cottage into a rather more comfortable one, with an orchard and a vegetable garden."

In a green flash he found himself back at home—but a home that was his mother's heart's delight. And a year passed by. One morning the people of the Lotus City were ordered to stay indoors.

"Her Serene Highness the Princess So-Shi is going to the Lotus Banks. No one may see her pass."

Aladdin felt his old adventurous spirit stir. He disguised himself as a fruit-seller and waited outside the baths. When the Princess arrived he held out to her the pressed petals of the jasmine flower she had given him.

She recognized him at once. "My father is still angry," she whispered. "Somehow, we must get his permission to marry."

Aladdin remembered the wonderful lamp which he had put away in a cupboard in his mother's kitchen.

"Leave it to me," he said.

But when he got home, he found that his mother had given the lamp away to a door-to-door salesman who had called offering new lamps for old.

"Foolish old fellow," said the widow. "Look, Aladdin, our new lamp polishes up beautifully."

"Mother," cried Aladdin. "That was no door-to-door salesman. You've given away the wonderful lamp to Abanazar. I must warn Princess So-Shi at once."

But Princess So-Shi had vanished. So had the Mandarin. So had his palace.

Despairingly, Aladdin twisted the ring on his finger.

"What are my master's commands?" said the Slave of the Ring.

"Where is the Princess? And Abanazar?"

"In Arabia, Master. The all-powerful Genie of the Lamp has spirited away the Princess, Mandarin, palace and all."

"Then take me to Arabia," said Aladdin.

"That I can do. I can help you no further."

"Yes you can. Make me a lute. Good. Now a flask full of opium. Good. And now make a plum tree grow in the courtyard of the palace as soon as the moon rises."

When the yellow moon rose, Aladdin hid in the branches of the flowering plum tree, and serenaded the Princess with his lute. When she opened her window he whispered to her and handed her the flask of opium.

And Princess So-Shi filled Abanazar's pipe with opium. He smoked contentedly until he fell into a profound and to him—a terrible dream.

In it he imagined that the lovely Princess had found the hiding place of the wonderful lamp. In his dream he saw her tip-toe to the window and hand the lamp to lean, hungry Aladdin who had climbed into the branches of a plum tree. He saw Aladdin rub the wonderful lamp. The genie sprang up as tall as the palace roof.

"Command—and I obey, Master."

When the wicked magician came out of his dream he found himself in the dungeon of the Mandarin's palace, thousands of miles from Arabia.

Needless to say, the Mandarin, safe in his palace in the Lotus City gladly agreed that the Princess So-Shi should marry Aladdin. To this day in the Lotus City they talk of the marvellous procession of boats, the lantern bearers and the feast that marked the wedding celebrations of Princess So-Shi and the poor widow's son, Aladdin.

How to catch a Leprechaun

Brian Boru, High King of Ireland, had two children, Shaun and Cathleen.

"Children," said the High King one day, "to rule the people you must understand the people—especially the Little People."

By the Little People he meant, of course, the Shee, the fairies. And of all the Shee the most mischievous were the leprechauns. Even Brian Boru, the High King himself, was plagued by them.

"By my crown and harp," he said, "they're the mischief. But with the luck of the Irish, children, you may catch one. And if you do, the leprechaun will give you three wishes sure to come true."

But the High King's children were perplexed.

"How do you catch a leprechaun, Shaun?" asked Cathleen.

"I don't know," said Shaun. "But I know who does—old Adam, the gardener."

"A trap for a leprechaun?" Old Adam leaned on the handle of his spade. "There's only one bait is sure to catch them. Potheen."

"What is potheen, Adam?" asked Shaun.

"Dew," said Adam, "gathered by moonshine—enough to fill a silver thimble."

So Cathleen approached her mother next morning.

"Mother," she said, "may I borrow your silver thimble?"

"Of course, my darling," came the reply.

That night, Shaun and Cathleen stole out into the rose garden and gathered by moonshine enough dew to fill the silver thimble. In the morning, they ran into the garden to Adam.

"Adam, Adam! We've got a silver thimble full of potheen. What do we do next?"

"Ask Colleen Bawn, the cook, for a jam-jar with a screw-on lid. And mind you prick a hole in the lid with a good strong darning-needle."

Colleen Bawn produced a jam-jar.

"Sure," she said. "Here it is. I washed it and dried it and polished it to fill it with new-made strawberry jam which I'm boiling at this minute in the brass preserving pan."

Shaun and Cathleen ran back to Adam.

"Adam," they cried, "we've got the

potheen in the silver thimble and the jam-jar with the screw-top lid and a darning-needle prick in the top. What do we do next?"

"Now for the tricky part," said Adam. "Leprechauns are sly and cunning. They have eyes at the back of their heads. If you try to catch them, the slightest shadow warns them and they're off and away. You must plant your trap an hour before high noon. At high noon the sun is straight above your head and casts no shadows.

"Borrow a dab of glue from the carpenter," he went on, "and stick your silver thimble full of potheen to the bottom of the jam-jar. Then cushion the bottom of the jar with rose petals."

"We'll get them at once," cried the children.

As they filled the bottom of the jam-jar with rose petals, they heard the sound of fairy laughter.

"Ha-ha-ha, hee-hee-hee.

Fill your jar—it won't catch me."

They looked all around them. The garden was full of roses, butterflies and velvet-brown bees droning from flower to flower. But they saw no leprechaun.

"Dig a hole," said old Adam, "just large enough to bury the jam-jar. Here's a good spot—close by this clump of lavender."

So Shaun and Cathleen scooped a hole close to the lavender clump and buried the jam-jar so that its mouth was just level with the soil.

"I'm tired, Cathleen," said Shaun when they had finished.

"So am I," said Cathleen and yawned. "Let's curl up and go to sleep in the sun. I don't believe a word of what old Adam has told us. Do you?"

"No I don't," said Shaun. "And I'll tell you something else. I don't believe in leprechauns either."

They stretched themselves out on the lawn near the clump of lavender and pretended to go to sleep. Slowly, slowly, the sun climbed higher and higher into the blue sky. The scent of the roses was sweet

in the drowsy noon-tide air. But the scent of the potheen in the silver thimble was sweeter. A small shadow flitted across the grass—the shadow of a little man all elbows and legs and lean body, like a daddy-long-legs. A shadow that jumped into the jam-jar.

"Quick, Cathleen," said Shaun. He pounced on the jam-jar and screwed on the lid.

There was a furious buzzing, like a dozen bumble-bees all buzzing together.

Shaun plucked the jam-jar from the ground. Inside it they both saw a streak of green flashing up and down. The streak moved so fast that at first it was just a blur of movement. Then it gradually slowed down and they saw the leprechaun.

The little man was about four inches in height. His body was long and thin. His face was long and pointed. His nose was long and pointed. His chin was long and pointed. His ears were long and pointed. His elbows were sharp, his knees were sharp and he was in a great paddywack.

The leprechaun's pointed hands had seven fingers and his pointed feet had nine toes. He clenched his fists and beat on the side of the jar.

"Let me out!" he screamed in a high, shrill voice. "Let me out or I'll put the curse of the black horse on the both of you."

"Oh no you won't," laughed Shaun. "We've caught you. And we won't let you go until you've granted us our three wishes."

The leprechaun glared at them through the glass. His eyes were scarlet and the thin line of his mouth worked with rage.

"Let me out! Let me out!"

"Not until you've granted us our wishes," said Cathleen.

All at once the leprechaun stopped beating the glass with his clenched fists. He sank to the bottom of the jam-jar and stretched his body on the rose petals.

"I'm dying, I'm dying," he gasped. "No air. Let me out."

"Poor little thing," said Cathleen. "Let him out, Shaun."

"Not I," said Shaun. "He's pretending. I

can see the wicked gleam in his scarlet eyes."

Instantly the leprechaun became a green streak again, flickering up and down between the roses and the screw-top of the jar.

"You can keep up that caper as long as you like," said Shaun. "We shan't let you out until we get our three wishes."

The afternoon shadows were beginning to lengthen in the garden before the leprechaun stopped being a streaky blur of green and became again a little man dressed all in green, with seven fingers on each hand and nine toes on each foot.

"I give in," he sobbed. "You can have your three wishes."

"You wish first, Cathleen," said Shaun.

"Father always told me," said Cathleen, "that a true princess should be able to hold her head high and proud but should also be better than ordinary women at all the things they do. I wish I could cook anything I want to, but especially Irish stew fit to put before the High King himself."

"So you shall," said the leprechaun, "when you let me out."

"I wish," said Shaun, "that I could play the harp of Tara better than my father's harper."

"So you shall," said the leprechaun, "when you let me out."

Cathleen clapped her hands and Shaun unscrewed the lid of the jam-jar.

Like a long streak of lightning the leprechaun leaped from the jar.

"I can't wait to make that Irish stew!" cried Cathleen. "Come on, Shaun. You play the harp to inspire me."

"So I will," said Shaun, "but I must have the biggest helping when you've cooked it."

"That's not fair," cried Cathleen. "Adam the gardener should have that for teaching us how to catch a leprechaun."

"Sure, now," said Adam, "and I'll be making today a high day and a feast day. And don't you forget that, between the two of you, you've each got half a wish to come."

As to what they did with their two half wishes, by the gold harp of Tara that's another story entirely.

King Grizzly Beard

Of all the fairytale princesses, Dagmar of Bohemia was probably the proudest and most disdainful. Every morning when she got up, her mirror whispered to her:

"You are more beautiful than Snow White or Rose Red."

Dagmar believed the mirror—and in fact it was a very truthful mirror, for she *was* very beautiful. But what the mirror told her made Dagmar so vain and conceited that she was almost unbearable to everyone at court, including even her father and mother.

Nevertheless, because she was so dazzlingly lovely, princes from all over Europe came to woo her. No matter how important or handsome or good they were, Dagmar spurned them all.

One day a very important person indeed came to woo Dagmar. He was not a prince, but a real, fully-qualified king. He was tall, dark, very handsome, and he wore a beard. Because it was so bushy he was nicknamed "King Grizzly Beard".

The conceited Princess treated him with even colder contempt than she had treated all her other would-be lovers. (Though secretly she thought him by far the most good-looking of them all.) The King and Queen liked him very much. They thought he would be a most suitable husband for their daughter.

King Grizzly Beard stayed at the court for several weeks. He paid the Princess the most flattering compliments, and he gave her the most rich and rare presents: a white peacock, a ring made from a piece of gold stolen from the Rhine Maidens; a magic harp which needed no human fingers to play it.

"You are wasting your time, Your Majesty," said Princess Dagmar. "Go away. You bore me."

"Very well, lovely and disdainful Princess," said the King at last. "When I have taken leave of your parents I will ride back to my own kingdom and try to forget you."

The King and Queen were furious with Dagmar.

"Dagmar is wrong in her head," cried her mother. "King Grizzly Beard would have made her an ideal husband."

"I couldn't agree more, my love," said the King. "He was the richest as well as the most handsome of her suitors. By the brightest jewel in my crown, I'll give Dagmar's hand in marriage to the first civil-spoken young man who turns up at court."

Next evening, a wandering minstrel arrived at the palace. He was poorly dressed, but he entertained the court with songs, ballads and snatches and the King said:

"Minstrel, we thank you for a pleasant evening. You may have our daughter's hand in marriage."

"No," cried Princess Dagmar. "No, no, no."

"Yes, yes, yes," shouted her father.

The very next morning Princess Dagmar and the wandering minstrel were married by the archbishop in the private chapel of the palace. After the wedding breakfast the unhappy couple were given a cold send-off by the courtiers, all of whom were very tired of the Princess's airs.

"I only have a mule, my dear," said the minstrel. "His name is Jennet." He helped his bride into the very uncomfortable saddle and led her out of the courtyard. The Princess gave a stifled sob.

"Where are we going?" she asked.

"To my home, of course. *Our* home from now on. It's many miles away and a poor sort of place when we get there. But at least it has a roof and four more or less rainproof walls. I'm not a rich man, like the other ones who have been courting you. But at least we shall have one another, even if we haven't much else."

Princess Dagmar began to weep.

"Now then, dear heart," said the minstrel, "We can't do with tantrums. You'll have to get used to the idea of leading a simple life."

Towards nightfall they came to a miserable-looking hut in a forest clearing.

"Here we are. Home," said the minstrel. "I don't know about you but I'm hungry. Go in and light the fire and make me some sort of a supper."

The Princess had never lit a fire in her life and the minstrel had to show her how to start it off with little twigs, then larger ones and finally still larger ones.

"I'll do it for you just this once," he said. "From tomorrow onwards you'll have to get up first and have a blazing wood fire for me when I get up."

"What about supper?" asked the Princess. "Where are the servants?"

"Servants?" asked the minstrel. "You must be joking. There's the cooking pot. Fill it with water from the well, add two handfuls of thick oatmeal, stir, keep on stirring and don't forget a small pinch of salt. Luckily, we've got about half a pint of blue skimmed milk to make the porridge taste better."

The Princess stirred the porridge so clumsily that the oatmeal became thick with large lumps which broke when spooned up and spread dry uncooked flour, made less appetizing still by the skimmed milk.

"I can't eat this," cried the Princess. "I'm used to dainty dishes. Jellies and blancmanges, delicious pancakes, omelettes made with three eggs, lemon meringue pies, eccles cakes simply stuffed with muscatels, currants and sultanas and coated with brown sugar. Not horrible food like this."

"Don't worry too much," said the minstrel. "About once a month I take to the road on a mule, am well received at a castle and in return for my songs I get a good supper. In about five weeks time I'll be off and for your sake I'll manage to hide some of the good food in a red and white spotted handkerchief and bring it home for you. Which reminds me, tomorrow you must wash my best minstrel's shirt, dry it on the grass, iron it and press my second best trousers so that I can make a good impression wherever I go."

He kissed her and went out to the stable, saying, "I'll be back when I've fed and watered Jennet the mule."

But he didn't return for three weeks. All the Princess had to live on was a binful of oatmeal and whatever skim milk she could persuade her neighbour the swineherd's wife to lend her—which wasn't much. Still, she gradually learned to make the horrible oatmeal porridge just about smooth and less dry and floury.

Towards the end of the third week a small, scruffy, ragged little boy knocked at the back door and handed the Princess a torn and dirty screw of paper.

"No answer needed, mum," he said and ran off.

The Princess unscrewed the paper and read the few scrawled words:

"Dear Wife

Hope this finds you better than it leaves me. Not a successful trip. Was falsely accused of stealing a gold ring from the Baron de Ratz. Am in dungeon awaiting trial. Have managed to smuggle this out. Hope you are learning more about cookery. Your ever-loving husband."

Before the Princess had time to take in

this sad news, a fat man in a three-cornered hat rapped at the door.

"I'm the magistrate's bailiff," he said. "I arrest you in the name of the law."

He marched the Princess off to court. When the Princess told the magistrate her name was Princess Dagmar, the magistrate banged angrily on the bench.

"You must think I've taken leave of my senses," he barked. "You, a princess? You're the wife of that rascal of a minstrel who stole a gold ring from the Baron de Ratz. I know very well he smuggled it to you by the hand of a ragamuffin of a boy. Don't dare contradict me. You shall be flung into a dungeon and live on very salty water and very old bread until your husband can earn enough money to release you. It will take him about seven years, I should think."

The Princess shrieked but she was taken down hundreds of steps and locked in a dungeon. The dungeon was dark, damp and had only one barred window, very small, near the ceiling. There were rustling sounds and to her horror, a rat ran over the damp straw which was all the dungeon had to offer by way of a bed.

After three days and nights the warder opened the dungeon door.

"Out," he barked. "Orders."

"What are you going to do to me?" sobbed the Princess.

"Me? Nothing," said the warder. "It's what *They* will do to you that you've got to worry about. Come on. Step lively."

The Princess was led into a wonderful room, its walls hung with tapestries and silks and satins, its richly carpeted floor strewn with sumptuous cushions. Two maids took off the Princess's now very ragged and tattered clothes. They led her to a bath, washed away all the grime of the dungeon and dressed her in the kind of clothes she had been accustomed to all her life—before the wandering minstrel married her.

When the Princess tried to ask them what it all meant they made signs to show that they were dumb. Then they led the bemused Dagmar into a stately hall. There were two thrones on a raised platform at the end of the hall. On one sat King Grizzly Beard, in royal robes and a glittering golden crown.

"My love," he said, stepping down from the throne and taking her by the hand. "Why—good gracious me. You're weeping."

"I can't help it," sobbed Dagmar. "Oh, my dear, dear love, I've dreamed about you very night in that awful dungeon."

"Ah," said King Grizzly Beard. "It was too bad of me to have taught you so severe a lesson."

"My love," sobbed the Princess. "It's too late. I should never have sent you away so cruelly. Now we can never be married. My father gave my hand in marriage to a wretch of a wandering minstrel."

The King stroked his great grizzly beard.

"Did he, now?" he asked. Then he smiled. "And am I to blame him? I was that wandering minstrel. Just as I was the warder and the magistrate. Your pride and vanity drove me to take extreme measures. But all the time I loved you too well to lose you. These apparently cruel acts were just meant to teach you a little about life—and how other people less fortunate than you have to manage. How they have to scrimp and save and manage somehow to live happy and useful lives. But come, it is all over now. And so, I hope, is your pride."

So the misfortunes of the proud and disdainful Princess were over. But she *had* learned her lesson. As King Grizzly Beard's queen she became famous for her goodness, kindness and complete lack of pride. And to tell you a secret only the palace cook shared, at least once a week Queen Dagmar would slip down to the kitchen, put on a plain but becoming and practical apron with big pockets and act as kitchen maid to the royal cook. In due time she became a better pastrycook, with a lighter hand on a rolling pin, than the cook herself. And little did King Grizzly Beard realize, when he raised the cook's salary after a particularly delicious angel cake, that it had been made by the hands of his own Queen.